# The 1776 Bed and Breakfast

By Louise Harris

D1523777

Second  printing

All characters in this book are fictitious, and any resemblance to real
persons, living or dead, is coincidental.

ISBN: 978-1-4489-8947-8

Printed in the United States of America

This book is dedicated to my mother and father who owned a bed and breakfast in Cape May, N.J. Thank you for years of inspiration for this book. Thank you for all your hard work to get me where I am today.

# Chapter 1
*Tourist Season Opens*

The wind chilled Angelique as she stood on the balcony of the bed and breakfast she owned. She always got a chill when she gazed at the Delaware River even on a warm spring day as this one was. It constantly reminded her of the day the flood took her father, an officer in the Coast Guard. She vowed never to have anything to do with water. Yet, here she was the owner of a Philadelphia bed and breakfast that overlooked the river.

Angelique returned to her bedroom, quickly dressed and fled down the steps to her freedom. She welcomed the warmth, especially after the long winter. Angelique barely made ends meet because few guests stayed at her place in the winter. *Now I can start making a profit again with the spring and summer tourist season here at last.*

The sun melted the last remaining ice particles on sidewalks while Angelique followed the river. She observed water fowl looking to mate, boats chugging, runners preparing for a marathon, and people like herself out for a walk.

At Penn's landing, she halted. Near the dock was a Coast Guard ship. Next to that was a private fishing boat, a private shipping company, and a tour boat. Just then, someone running for the dock barreled into Angelique knocking her on the ground.

"Hey! Watch where you are going!" she shouted.

Offering a hand to help her back to her feet, Buck Robertson answered, "I'm sorry. I am late for work."

Then, he left without checking if Angelique was well. She saw him run the remaining distance to the pier. Despite his rudeness, Angelique noticed him as he ran. His tall, broad figure with sandy brown hair burned in her memory. She could not let go of those thoughts despite her attempts. Angelique walked for another hour before heading back to her inn. When she arrived, Maggie had breakfast waiting on the dining room table. Angelique ate a banana nut muffin.

"Ah hope your muffin is to ye likin'," the black housekeeper said.

"It's fine."

"Where ya go? Philadelphia's no place for a young lady alone."

"I took a walk. I needed air. I've been cooped up too long this winter. I'm under stress. And, where I go is none of your business. You are an employee."

That last comment came out too harshly, but Angelique still fumed about the earlier incident. Actually, she considered Maggie more of a friend than an employee. She confided in Maggie when no one else cared about her feelings.

"I'm sorry, Maggie. I didn't mean it. Someone knocked into me, and it must have troubled me more than I thought."

Angelique caught the smile on Maggie's face. She knew what the housekeeper thought. That she was moody and prone to outbursts. That she was impulsive and needed protecting. Maggie had lived with the 21-year-old all her life. She was nine years older than Angelique and became her great comforter when her French parents died in her teens. Angelique disliked this motherly attitude because at the time of their deaths, Maggie's mother was still alive to take care of her. But, Maggie often looked after her too. Angelique smiled as she remembered Maggie's mother waiting for her when she got home from school. Now, Maggie was the only family Angelique had left.

* * *

As Buck ran, he saw the woman's shiny black hair flowing in the breeze. Her hazel eyes sparkles against the sun. He also remembered her cheeks that blossomed into little roses because of her anger. He even liked her height. He took pleasure in these thoughts as he ran, but they quickly disappeared when he reached the office.

"Reporting for work."

"You're late," bellowed Franklin Kennedy, the cruise line's owner. "When I hired you as manager, I thought you would be punctual. Every minute you're late, I lose money. I can't lose money. I need every dollar I can get. Got that?"

"Yes, sir."

Buck worked for the Delaware River Touring Co., a business that offers tours of the river to the Delaware Bay and

back again.

"Good. Here are your bookings for the week."

"How come the tour on Saturday stays at the bay for more than an hour? This is supposed to be a three-hour tour," Buck said.

"It's a special. I've given an extra two hours for the price of three. They can watch for dolphins."

"Dolphins don't come until August. The water is too cold."

"This is my ship. I can do as I please. Now get to work!"

Buck was suspicious of the owner's desire to have the ship at the bay for two extra hours, but he did not press the issue further. He did not want to get him angrier. Mr. Kennedy stormed from the office.

The touring company's office sat next to the pier. The main lobby had shelves of information about Philadelphia and a ticket counter where a girl sat and a room to the right which was Buck's office. In the lobby, three benches filled the cramped space.

Passengers crowded the benches. They were so tight they could barely breathe. Most of them carried cameras and wore 1776 T-shirts and long pants. The crew appeared in blue and white sailor outfits, long navy pants for the men and navy skirts for the women. Most passengers were excited for the trip. The crew, however, showed signs of a company not well-run, poor morale and anger. All of the crew scowled, wore uniforms with holes in them, and slouched against the walls. Buck could see from her expression that the girl at the desk wished she was
somewhere else, but like the crew, she needed the job and put up with the poor company to get money to pay rent. Buck shook his head when he saw her.

Buck welcomed the tourists and his crew. Some tourists could not speak English. The girl at the ticket counter started to take money for the reservations. She could speak French, Spanish and English and translated. Her brown hair with blonde highlights was pulled into a pony tail. Buck left for the
manager's room.

When he was alone in his office, Buck had a stack of paperwork to do. He could not help thinking about the woman he knocked on the ground. *Oh she'll never want to know me after I was so rude. I don't even know her name or where to find her.* Buck began to plow through the mound of paperwork, calculating receipts, checking manifests, ordering food for the dinners and lunches, logging the trips, checking payroll and recording in the accounting books. Right now, he was a manager, but that was only temporary. His retired parents would be proud of him.

* * *

"Maggie, where is my guest book?"

"Ah saw it in kitchen."

"I want to make a nice display up front with it. The spring tourist season has begun."

"Don't worry, Miss. I'll get it. Maybe, ya should sit, instead o' wearing rug thin."

"I don't know why I'm pacing. All of a sudden, I can't sit still. I'm worried about making money this season."

"Don't ya always make money when it's warm, especially on the 4th of July?"

"Yes, but this winter was especially hard. If I don't bring in some money soon, I don't know what I'll do."

"I know, Miss. Don't ya worry. The reception will work for ya. It always does."

Angelique held a party every year to open the tourist season. All the top people in town were invited. They always came. They always recommended her inn to their friends, co-workers, family and associates. She had a similar event at Christmas, on New Year's Eve and at the end of the summer.

"Maggie, did you deposit this week's receipts into the bank?"

"Ah started to go, but Ah couldn't find where Ah put it."

"You didn't deposit the money?" Angelique frowned. She was worried.

"Don't worry. Ah'll go when Ah find it. The money must be here somewheres."

"The money is missing? Keep searching. I can't afford to lose any money."

"Don't worry."

Despite Maggie's reassurances, the missing money bothered Angelique. She could not think about it now. She had to concentrate on the party.

# Chapter 2
## *The Reception*

Angelique entered the bedroom and opened her closet to get ready for the evening reception. She put on white pantyhose and a spaghetti-strap blue gown with sequins down the front she bought at a thrift shop. She wore a sapphire and diamond necklace that belonged to her mother. She strapped black shoes with high heels to her ankles. She styled her hair. One black wave would not give up its fight to fall on her face. She let it stay. *Oh well. No one will notice.*

Knock. Knock.

"Come in."

"Just bringin' your towels, Miss. That's a sexy dress. Those shoes show off your legs."

"Thank you, Maggie."

"Maybe ya can find an eligible man at your reception."

"You are always asking me to find a man. Why?"

"Ya always look lonely."

"Well, most of the men that come to my receptions are married. And I'm perfectly happy alone."

"If ya say so."

Angelique shot Maggie a look and left to do the finishing touches for her party. She opened the door for the band and caterer and showed them where to go. Maggie and the other employees wore black and white uniforms. The inn hired the same florist who decorated City Hall for events. The florist provided bouquets that stood three-feet tall with purple orchids, cream colored gardenias, yellow-colored carnations and coral-colored roses. The orchid and gardenia aromas filled the room. She asked her staff to start a fire in the fireplace, which brought a homey feeling to the room. Angelique scanned the room. Everything was perfect. She was tying the last of the purple and gold bows on the fireplace mantle when Maggie entered.

"Are ya mad at me? Ya seem upset," she said.

"No. Just nervous about tonight. I don't want anything to go wrong."

"Ya parties always turn out OK."

That had been true in the past, but this time, Angelique had a bad feeling. She shrugged, thinking it was her nerves. Angelique greeted her guests as they arrived. She met executives of banks, stars and owners of Philadelphia sports teams, leaders of the hospitality industry, lawyers and vice presidents of development companies. The mayor and his wife accepted the invitation this year. Angelique's cousin who served in Congress decided to come as well. Maggie checked their coats.

The catering staff butlered shrimp, cheese puffs and mini-quiches. The band softly played songs from Philadelphia artists. Angelique requested a variety of music types. Although she was talking to her guests, her mind kept turning to that mysterious man who had plowed into her. She wondered if she would see him again. Sometimes, she smiled about that prospect, which confused the guests who thought she laughed at a depressing story. She enjoyed herself and relaxed a little.

Many more people attended this year's reception than last year's. The guests enjoyed themselves. They freely talked to each other, drank wine and ate the food. She hoped the reservations would begin coming.

"These quiche are fabulous," the mayor's wife told Angelique.

"Thank you. I always use this caterer. She takes great care with all her food and presentations."

"I'll have to consider her for one of our parties."

"Let me get you her number."

* * *

Meanwhile, at 7 o'clock, Buck assembled his workers for the night cruise. He talked to them about good attitudes when handling tourists. They rolled their eyes as if they had heard it a thousand times. He knew they thought he would not last long as their manager. The last three managers left under suspicious circumstances. He ignored their looks and finished his speech. He was about to tell the ship's captain to cast off when Mr. Kennedy appeared.

"Robertson," he yelled. "Here." Mr. Kennedy handed Buck a ticket.

"What's this?"

"I can't go. You have to go to represent the cruise line."

"A reception at the 1776 Inn?"

"Yes. We do a lot of business with that B&B. She refers her tourists to us. Make a good impression. Get going!" he yelled."Why is the ship still here? It's costing me money every moment it sits at dock." Buck clenched his fists and flexed his muscles.

"Yes, sir." He wanted to punch his boss, but he knew he had to acquiesce for now. "Captain, go."

Buck looked at the ticket. The reception started at 7:30 p.m. He did not have time to change. His navy business suit would have to do.

When he arrived, Angelique said, "Welcome to the 1776 Inn's Annual Spring Reception."

"Thank you."

"You look familiar. Have you been to my reception before?"

"No. But you're right. I've met you somewhere."

"Now I remember. Aren't you the idiot who knocked me down?"

Buck said, "I guess I am."

The smirk annoyed her. "Don't you want to know how I am? Or don't you care about how you treat women?"

"Forgive my manners. Why don't we start over. My name is Bonneville Robertson, but everybody calls me Buck. I would like to get to know you better. I hope I didn't hurt you in any way the other day."

"No, not physically." *You are the most handsome man I've ever met.* "Angelique Chalfonte."

"You look beautiful in that dress."

"Thank you." Quenching the fire stirring inside her, she added, "So where do you work?"

"I work for the Delaware River Touring Co. The cruise line needed a manager. I needed a job, so I applied."

"Just like that? Sounds pretty cold."

"I guess."

"Don't you look into a company before applying?"

"Not when I have rent to pay. I understand that you send tourists our way."

"Yes we do." She shivered at the thought of the owner. "But, sometimes, I hear complaints about the tours."

Buck shrugged. "I'll look into that."

"Aren't you afraid the ship will capsize or something?" Her voice trembled when she asked that question.

"It's a three-hour tour down the Delaware. Couldn't be more safe. We don't even go out in bad weather. Why don't you take a trip?"

"I can't. I have an inn to run."

"OK, but you're missing a beautiful sunset over the bay."

"You've gone on tour then?"

"No. I just started my job this week. I've heard about it, though. Actually, as manager, I don't go out on the river much."

"If you don't go on the tour, why are you saying I should go?" She frowned.

"Because I think you are judging something as bad before you try it." She saw the quizzical expression on his face.

"No. I'm not. I just have other things to do."

"There must be some time you can get away for yourself?" Buck encouraged.

"Not really. Besides, I just don't want to go."

"How can you recommend it without trying it?"

"You're right. Maybe, I shouldn't recommend it."

"That's not what I meant. I think you would enjoy yourself."

"You are awfully pushy." Angelique didn't like this conversation. She wanted it done.

"I'm sorry. I didn't mean to offend you," Buck said.

"You didn't. Why do you think I would enjoy myself if you haven't gone?"

"I don't know. But I like to try new things before I judge them."

Angelique thought he was rude. "Excuse me. I have to tend to the other guests."

"Sure. I hope you take me up on my invitation."

"We'll see." Her voice cracked. She wanted to go on the trip because she liked him despite his rudeness, but her fears won't let her go. She watched Buck flirt with other single women at the party.

She couldn't understand why this would upset her so much. *I just met this man and he works on the river.* She decided to ignore Buck for the rest of the night. *He is perfectly entitled to talk to whomever he wishes.*

One of the women carried wine and a plate full of quiche. She tried to move past Buck and tripped. She spilled the wine and quiche on his suit. The shock caused Buck to stumble and fall into Angelique who ripped her dress on the fireplace poker. The rip exposed her breasts and lacy underwear. Buck helped her to her feet.

"Are you all right?"

"Look at me."

"Gladly," he said as he choked back the laughter and filled his eyes with her beauty and nakedness.

Angelique's annoyance over this man came back to her. Trying to cover up the unexpected exposure, she said, "Why are you laughing?"

"I can't help it. The situation is funny."

"No it isn't!" Her voice got louder.

"Yes it is."

Angelique looked at her guests who were staring at her. Some, like Buck, laughed. Others pitied her.

"Buck, you wouldn't think it was funny if it happened to you."

"I wouldn't be wearing a revealing dress."

"I meant if you ripped your pants or something, you jerk!" she shouted above the music. "I never want to go on your boat!" She waved the fireplace poker in the air. She paced. It seemed like hours but was really only a minute or two.

In minutes, Maggie brought Angelique a coat and quickly buttoned it. She felt the stares from the guests who no longer pitied her and stomped away from him and the guests. She hid in a corner until everyone left and could not enjoy herself at the party after that. At midnight, when everyone was gone, Angelique climbed up to bed. She decided she needed to do something to retaliate against the manager at the Delaware River Touring Co. *That manager is no better than his boss. He laughed at me. Laughed at me! He is so rude. I'm foolish to think about him all the time.* When she fell asleep in her bed, she dreamed about a man with sandy brown hair who escorted her on a gambling ship to land on a deserted beach.

*Stupid. Stupid. Stupid. I didn't handle that well, but she was so gorgeous. I couldn't not look.*

Right after Angelique stomped away, Buck stood wondering what he could to make Angelique less angry. He decided it did not matter. He spoke with a few guests before slipping out the door unnoticed. He trudged back to his office. It was 10:30. He did not want to go home. He sat at his desk and stared through the small window overlooking the Delaware. He remembered scanning her body. She was so beautiful. *I have to get her out of my head. She doesn't like me.*

Buck tried to remove her presence by working on the accounting databases. Looking at the numbers logged into the software, he noticed a mistake. *That can't be right. The revenues are off. I must have added wrong. I'm tired. It's too late in the day to worry about it. I'll let it go for now. I will check in the morning.*

When the ship returned at 11, Buck managed the docking, filed the manifest and left for home at midnight.

# Chapter 3
## *The Letter*

The next morning, Angelique woke to anxiety pains in her stomach. The previous night had been a complete disaster. She wondered how she could recover from such a blunder. She would surely lose recommendations after those executives saw her nearly naked. Without those recommendations, she would lose revenue. She had to fix this before it became too late, but Angelique didn't know how. She couldn't have another reception. No one would come. Besides, she had spent a great deal on that one.

Angelique lay on her pillow thinking of how to counteract the negative publicity she would receive. She couldn't think of anything. *This is all that man's fault. He made my dress rip. If he had never come last night, I would not be in this mess.* She vowed to protect her inn's diminishing reputation. Soon, Angelique had an idea to sever ties with Delaware River Touring Co., its owner and its manager. She began a letter. Having made that decision, she felt better. Angelique dressed and glanced at the weather. It was raining, which made her gloomy. She walked into the kitchen where Maggie cleaned the counters.

"What can Ah get ya?" Maggie asked.

"Just tea. I'm not hungry."

"Ya need to eat."

"Later."

"Not good for ya to not eat."

"Maggie, you're not my mother. I'll get something later."

"Right. That was some party last night."

"Don't talk to me about that party."

"What ya goin' to do?"

"I don't know yet." She changed the subject.

"Maggie, do you know why I hate rain?"

"It reminds ya of the day your dad died?"

She threw Maggie a scornful look. "It reminds me of the dreariness in society."

"Right."

"Besides, it's bad for business."

"Ya mean it reminds ya of people who do bad things to ya."

"That's not true."

"Ya weren't happy about what they did to ya last night."

"The rain is not making me think of those people."

"I see. What's wrong with rain? It brings flowers. And rainbows. And new life."

Maggie could always see the good side to everything, Angelique thought. She never sees rain as destruction or despair. If it hadn't rained that day, Angelique's parents might be alive.

"What good came from THAT rainy day?" Angelique knew Maggie would understand which day she meant.

"Good always comes from tragedies. My mother became your guardian until ya left school. We became friends. Ya were given the inn and money to run it," Maggie said. Angelique stared at her.

"I wanted to travel after I graduated, but instead, I had to come here and run the inn."

"But ya love the inn now. Ya always talk about being there for the guests and helpin' people enjoy themselves."

"True." Angelique softened. She remembered how she started the receptions to bring in extra revenue when her parents' savings disappeared. She loved meeting the leaders of society and talking to new faces every year. The receptions always worked except last night's. Her disposition fell again.

"Rain makes me so depressed. I can't cope on days like this. Today, I'm feeling worse after last night's fiasco."

"The rain might not bother ya if ya had a man."

"There you go again," Angelique sighed.

"Ya would look at life differently."

"I doubt that."

"Well if ya found the right one, ya would."

"Who do you think is the right one?" Angelique poured the tea.

"Someone who cares for ya and protects ya."

"Is that all?" Angelique folded her arms.

"And provides for ya."

She didn't like this conversation and asked sarcastically,

"What about love? Don't you think that's important?"

"That goes without sayin'."

"Oh and I suppose you know what love feels like?" she asked more sarcastically.

"Me? I know no one."

"My point exactly. Don't lecture me, OK?"

"Just bein' a friend."

"I know." She turned her back on Maggie. She was not about to let her know about the man at the dock that keeps occupying her mind. She certainly would rather see him drowned in the river but she couldn't stop thinking about him. He was so handsome. Maggie would surely make that into something it's not.

"Ya seem to light up when ya met that man last night."

"I'm not interested in him."

"Oh? Why?"

"He's rude."

"Sounds like ya should talk to 'im."

"I'm not having anything to do with him."

"Suit yerself. I'm going to clean rooms now."

"Bye," she said.

Angelique took the bread basket full of muffins and brought them to the dining room. She put the box of exotic teas on the table and filled the carafe with coffee. She provided plates, utensils, napkins, honey, lemons and cream. As she busied herself she thought about the rain and the river. Every time she saw the river, especially on rainy days, Angelique got that familiar sick feeling in her stomach. She could never get involved with someone who loved the river and grinned at the thought of severing ties with the touring company. Angelique caught up with Maggie on the second floor.

"When you're done on this floor, could you mail this letter. Send it certified. I want to make sure it is received. Get a return receipt."

"What's so important about it?"

"I sent a letter telling the Delaware River Touring Co. I have stopped our referrals."

"That could backfire. The owner could turn around and tell his business associates not to come to the inn."

"A risk I will have to take."

"Ya already could lose money from last night's party."

"I know. But we'll manage."

"Well, if ya sure, Ah'll mail it."

"Good. Now there will be no more talk about that man."

"Right."

"By the way, I am trying to arrange a meeting with the

Philadelphia Convention and Visitor's Bureau. I will call over there later today and set something up for later in the week. When I'm gone, you'll tend to the guests?"

"Of course, Miss."

* * *

That same morning, Buck woke in his two-room apartment in center city. He showered, ate his eggs and bacon and read the newspaper.

**Embezzlement Rate Increases in Philadelphia**, the headline read. The article was about several companies finding their owners taking money from the profits to deceive investors and debtors. Company owners are using the funds for a range of illegal activities, the story said. The story interested Buck, but he did not know why.

He cut the article from the *Philadelphia Bulletin* and placed the story in his vest. *I might need this some day.* It rained heavily, and wind blew through umbrellas. He had to get to work early to cancel scheduled trips. The gusts almost blew him away. He could not control his opened umbrella, struggling to stay balanced against the wind. Rain hit his coat like ice pellets instead of spring drops. *This is insane. I should turn around and go back home.* Yet, he continued trudging through the bad weather and reached the SEPTA station. He hopped on the El and rubbed his shoulders to regain some warmth. The morning rush hour meant the train was wall to wall people all soaking wet and carrying umbrellas. The bell sounded the arrival of Buck's destination. Once again, Buck fought the wind and rain all the way to his office near the river.

"We have to cancel today's tours," Buck said to the woman working at the ticket counter. "The weather is too dangerous."

"Yes, sir. Shall I hold off the evening's tours in case the weather improves?" she asked.

"That's a good idea. By the way, what is your name?"

"Roxanne Stevens. You can call me Roxy."

"Thank you, Roxy. You can call me Buck."

"What about refunds?"

"If they paid in advance, refund their money."

"No." Franklin Kennedy appeared at the door wearing a black-hooded raincoat and smiling a devious grin. He had a scar on his face. "We don't refund money."

"But sir, the weather. We can't take the tours today."

"It's just a little rain. We sail as planned. Is it our fault, it's raining? We didn't know it was going to rain when the customers booked."

Kennedy closed the door behind him. Buck did not like his choices. Going out in this weather was dangerous, but not giving refunds would anger customers who probably wouldn't book another tour. He sighed and said, "Close the top deck and sail as scheduled."

"But sir..."

"Roxy, you heard him. That is my final word."

Buck jumped when the door opened again. He did not want another encounter with Mr. Kennedy, but the wind had opened the door. Leaks on the roof sent a steady stream of rain down to Buck's desk. He opened a closet and took out a janitor's bucket, which he placed on his desk to capture the rain. When it overflowed, he dumped the bucket of water down the drain. The rain hit the rest of the roof, sounding like a snare drum. While he watched the stream of water above him, Buck imagined Angelique stood there. He saw her silky skin radiating through the water pellets in his office. It kept him going through the dismal conditions.

* * *

Heavy rains continued for several days, but the real storm came in Buck's office. The door swung open, forcing Buck to spring to his feet. Franklin Kennedy in his black suit and wet coat stood in front of him ready for war. Buck backed against the window and kept the desk between them when Mr. Kennedy spoke.

"I just received a letter from Ms. Chalfonte. She said she is refusing to recommend our tours to her guests. I thought I told you to shmooze her during that reception of hers."

"Yes, sir. I went." Buck stood his ground. He wasn't going to be intimidated by Kennedy.

"Then why is she not recommending my touring company?"

"I don't know."

"What happened?"

"Well, she got angry with me."

"Damn! Do you know how much money I'll lose?"

"No, sir." The storm grew louder, but Buck was not sure it was the rain or the thunder in the room. Buck's muscles tightened. He had to hold his temper in front of Kennedy.

"Lots. I expect you to fix it. Get her recommendation. I don't care if you have to sleep with her to do it." Buck looked shocked.

With that, he left. Not even giving Buck time to answer. *How can I fix this? I can't lose this job. I have a mission. I have to find a way out of this mess. Why did he tell me to sleep with her?*

Buck decided to talk to Angelique. He was not sure why she sent the letter, but he decided that as a businesswoman, she must be open to reason and logic. Buck peered out the window. He felt cramped in the office. Battling the elements seemed preferable to feeling like a sardine. He donned his already wet coat and grabbed umbrella and left. Walking aimlessly, Buck did not see the soft bank until it gave way. He slipped and dangled at the edge of the river.

"Help! Help! Help!"

"Hang on! I'll try to help!" Buck knew the voice. He knew Angelique was rescuing him. That gave him hope. He could barely see her, but he could see her hand. He grabbed it. He wasn't sure she was strong enough to get him to safety, but she managed surprisingly well. She pulled him onto the bank. He fell on top of her, knocking her backwards into the mud. She was soaked and covered in brown goo. Buck watched her umbrella float away in a stream of water in the street. He saw her eyes briefly dance with laughter before she frowned at him.

"I'm sorry," Buck said when he stood to get off her, not before brushing against her breast and feeling the softness there.

"It's OK. Are you all right?" she said with an air of concern.

"My arm hurts."

"What happened?" she asked as she tended to his arm.

"Ouch! I needed some air. I didn't see the soft bank."

"You should go to the medical center, but I don't think it's broken." She started looking in her bag for something.

"What are you doing out in this weather?" he asked as the pain in his arm showed across his face.

"I had an appointment with the Philadelphia Convention and Visitors Bureau."

"I hope it went well." He smiled at her.

"Maybe. You really should get your arm checked."

"I have to stay here and manage the tours." Buck tried to ignore the pain in his arm.

"Didn't you say you don't go out in bad weather?" A look of annoyance flashed across her face.

"I have no choice."

"That doesn't sound like good business."

"Mr. Kennedy's rules." He scowled. He didn't like those rules. He changed the subject. "As long as I have you here, I need to talk to you."

"What do you want to talk to me about?" she said casually.

"Why did you send Mr. Kennedy a letter not recommending our tours?"

"You just answered your question."

"I did?" he asked surprised.

"Yes. Your company puts people's lives at risk to make a few bucks," she said.

"That's not true."

"I've heard the complaints. And you're going ahead with today's tours despite these gusts and heavy rains."

"I told you I have no choice. You need to reconsider your recommendation."

"Why?"

"Because Kennedy is mad, and I could lose my job."

"I recommend your touring company. My guests get angry because they have to go out in weather like this or lose their money. Then they don't come back to my inn. I don't think so! I don't care whether you lose your job."

"Kennedy might retaliate." Buck was trying a new tactic.

"I expect him to get revenge, but I'll deal with it then."

"What is this letter really about?" He was annoyed with her.

"Meaning what?"

"Meaning that you are mad at me and taking it out on our company."

"I don't like you or your company. I don't want anything more to do with you."

Buck stood still as Angelique took out a rag. He watched her make a sling for his arm. He smiled at her but was shocked when she threw it at him. "You'll need this." He almost yelled after her when she ran, splashing in the puddles on her way back to the inn. He thought she liked him, but at that moment, he realized he blew it and that she wanted nothing to do with him.

Back in his office, Buck wondered why Kennedy was so insistent that the 1776 Inn help him. Surely, there were other inns to get business. He wondered why Kennedy wanted to go out in bad weather or why he insisted on sitting in the bay for hours. Buck planned to find out why these things were important to him. He gathered his crew together.

"We lost a major source of revenue today. To compensate, we will cut everyone's pay until we can find a revenue source to replace it. Anyone who calls out sick will be fired."

The workers groaned. Buck almost showed his agreement with the staff, but he had to maintain his authority.

"Also, I expect everyone to perform up to Delaware River Touring Company's standards or face the consequences."

Once again, the workers groaned. One said, "That's not fair."

"You're welcome to find another job if you like."

The worker looked at his feet. He wasn't going to protest any more. Compassion ran through Buck's heart, but he had a job to do. Kennedy's word was law around here.

"That's the way it has to be."

Buck saw the nods of agreement among the workers. In truth, he knew most needed the work and could not afford to lose it. Buck decided to use more compassion in his day-to-day judgment. He kept this information silent, though. He needed their help and confidence. Buck noticed the 18-year-old Roxy glaring. He wondered what she thought, but he suspected that Roxy, like the others needed the job. He knew she would not complain. Buck sat at his desk trying to find another place to recommend his tours and searched for ways to cut corners on the ships to offset costs.

# Chapter 4
## *The Fire*

*Dear Ms. Chalfonte,*

*Thank you for the invitation to your reception.*

*Although we enjoyed ourselves, we have decided that*

*the dignitaries expected for our spring festivals would*

*be better served at another place of lodging. We're*

*sorry for the inconvenience and hope you have a good*

*day.*

*Sincerely,*

*Carlotta Rizzo*

Angelique dropped the letter. Her heart sank. *How many more of these are going to come?* she wondered. She still hadn't heard from the convention and visitor's bureau. She mailed a press release about her inn to area newspapers and magazines, but so far reporters hadn't asked for an interview. As Angelique sat at her desk early in the evening thinking about what action she could take next to drum up some business, she stared out the window and saw the smoke. Something was on fire.

Angelique descended the stairs and hunted for Maggie. She found her in the drawing room helping a guest to tea.

"Maggie, did you see the smoke down the street?"

"No. Haven't looked out the window." Maggie went to the nearest window. "Oh my."

"I think it's the retirement complex. I'm going to go help."

"I'll call the fire department and stay with the guests," she said

.

"Good idea." Angelique filled jugs of water and grabbed some towels.

"Make sure ya don' get in the way."

As she walked, she heard the sirens blow. She offered water to the firefighters and the victims of the complex. Angelique stayed out of the firefighters' way, but she gave them help when they asked. She helped the residents find a safe place to stand and put towels around them. She soaked some wash cloths to wash away soot and grime. Angelique didn't touch the weaker residents but let the paramedics tend to them. Despite this, one resident came to her for help even though he was so weak.

"Here, drink some water."

The man said, "My son... Get word to him. He's all we have."

"I'll tell the firefighters. I'm sure they'll call anyone you want."

"Please. We need someone to tell him now." He coughed and collapsed on the ground.

Angelique looked at the weak man and decided to help him. She asked him for his son's name. His answer surprised her. She was holding the hand of Buck Robertson's father. The firefighters laid a woman next to him. Medical technicians tended to them. Both appeared in bad shape.

"I know him. I can get word to Buck, I mean, Mr. Robertson, for you," she said.

"Thank you."

Angelique saw the man settle back on the ground and close his eyes. She started crying because the horrible sight brought back memories of seeing her father so weak before he died. She pulled her cell phone from her purse.

"Buck, you have to come right away," she yelled into the phone. The retirement complex is on fire. Please come."

She rushed her words. She could tell Buck was confused.

"Why do you need me? The firefighters are there."

"Your parents. They're hurt."

"Both of them?"

"I'm not sure about your mother. I talked to your father who is weak. A woman was laid next to him unconscious."

"I see," he said.

"Are you coming?"

"No, I can't leave."

"Buck, they could die and all you can think about is keeping your job and making a profit for Mr. Kennedy? You should get over here now!"

"I'm sorry, Angelique."

The conversation made her curious. She couldn't understand Buck's attitude. At one point, she thought he was about to cry, but his voice returned to the cold, manner-of-fact conversation that made her angry. She closed her phone. The firefighters had rescued all the people from the complex. She saw one body with a sheet covering it. That made her sad. She prayed for the poor soul killed so tragically. Angelique headed back to her inn when she realized the firefighters didn't need any more help.

"Miss Angelique, ya look terrible," Maggie said.

"I know. I'm covered in soot."

"So what's goin' on?"

"The retirement complex looks completely gone. Smoke everywhere. A lot of people injured. One is dead." Angelique cried.

"What's wrong, Miss?" Maggie tapped her shoulder.

"I feel for those people."

"You is a good person."

"Do you know that one of the people asked me to call his son?"

"Yeah?"

"It turned out to be Buck, the manager of the Delaware River Touring Co.," she said to Maggie's unasked question.

"No kiddin'," Maggie said shocked. "Did ya call?"

"Yes. But I wish I hadn't."

"Why?"

"He wouldn't come to his parents' aid. He doesn't care enough about his own parents to leave work and be with them."

"Maybe, he had a reason."

"Oh, he had a reason. He didn't want to lose his job. I don't know what his problem is. I think family is more important than a job," Angelique explained.

"Family is important, but bills won't wait for family. Maybe, ya shouldn't be so hard on him. And, not everyone has the relationship you had."

Angelique didn't agree with her.

"The father desperately wanted his son there. Buck should have been there for his parents. It's not right for them to go through this alone."

"Maybe, ya could stay at the hospital with him—at least until the son can show up?"

"Good idea. Maggie, I have another. Tell the firefighters that any resident without anywhere to go, can stay here free of charge."

"Right."

Angelique put on her jacket, asked the police where the victims of the fire were taken and took the El there. She had to wait until the victims were given rooms. Mr. Robertson was put in a regular room while Mrs. Robertson was in intensive care. Angelique wasn't allowed to visit her.

"Mr. Robertson? Mr. Robertson?"

Blinking, he nodded. Angelique knew she had his attention. She grabbed his hand.

"I called your son, Buck. He said he'll see you as soon as he can. I will stay with you until he arrives."

Feeling apologetic for Buck, Angelique added, "He loves you."

Mr. Robertson smiled only faintly. He fell asleep. Angelique was told that Mrs. Robertson was in a coma. The long night took its toll on Angelique. She sat by Mr. Robertson's side and prayed for

him and his wife. Her hair lost
some of its shine and fell onto her face. She smelled the smoke on
her clothes, but she was determined to stay at the hospital
regardless of how long it took. Despair thickened the air. And she
thought she heard screams of pain coming from the room. After
looking at Mr. Robertson, Angelique realized she was mistaken.

Buck pounded his heart when he hung up the phone. He
loved his parents and did not want to see them die, especially if he
couldn't get to them in time. But, Mr. Kennedy's message about
employees clearly applied to Buck as well. If he left, Buck could lose
his job. He needed the job to finish his mission. His parents would
understand, but Buck wasn't sure Angelique would. He wanted to
tell her, but he couldn't. Buck wouldn't forgive himself if something
happened to his parents before he could tell them he loved them.
Just then, the phone rang. It was the administrator at the hospital.

"Mr. Robertson?"

"Yes?"

"I wanted to let you know that your parents are here. We
need your permission as next of kin to authorize treatments."

"Of course. Whatever you have to do. How are they?"

"We don't know yet, but your mother is unconscious. Your
father has a bad head injury and burns."

"Keep me posted." He gave the hospital his home, work and
cell phone numbers.

"We won't know anything until we begin treatment."

*Please God, spare them until I get there.* Buck tried to put his
parents out of his mind so he could get back to work, but it was

hard. Their lifeless bodies kept flashing before his eyes.

At the scene, he watched the flames, reveling in the dancing flickers. He enjoyed seeing the confused faces, the scared people, the death. The actions of the firefighters gave him a rush. He was excited. Everything about the fire pleased him. It reminded him of the fire he started as a boy. Everything was going according to plan.

"Sir, you have to move to a safe distance. The fire is out of control," the firefighter said.

The man did not answer but decided to leave. He picked a spot in the shadows where he could continue to watch.

# Chapter 5
## *The Morning After*

Before he left work, Buck check the public transportation schedule. He had to choose whether to take the last El to the hospital or his apartment. While waiting for the train, Buck punched in the number to the hospital. The administrator didn't know anything new and suggested he come in the morning. He decided to go home. His arm ached badly and he needed rest. In his apartment, Buck undressed and climbed into bed. He laid his head on the pillow but could not sleep. The pain from his arm, still in the sling, was unbearable even though he swallowed pain reliever tablets. His wide-awake mind kept bringing back the thought that his parents could die overnight. *I'll be there. Please wait. I love you.* Tears streamed down his face. Buck felt he abandoned them in their time of need. *They sacrificed everything and I repay them by not being by their side. How can I be so thoughtless?* He went into the bathroom and drank some water. Looking in the mirror, he washed his face. His ghostly colored skin had stains of tears and his five-o'clock shadow was darker than normal. "Everything would be OK," he said out loud. "I'll see them before work tomorrow."

Grabbing his bathrobe and wearing it over his boxer shorts and T-shirt, Buck walked around his apartment trying to relax so he could sleep. He dug out his baby blanket from his dresser.

When his phone rang, he jumped. It was 12:30. He was sure it was the hospital calling. He was relieved when he heard Roxy's voice.

"Buck?"

"Yes."

"Good. I got your number from the Internet. I was hoping it was the right one. I wanted to know if you wanted company."

"Roxy, you're nice and all, but you're too young for me."

"No, Buck. I don't mean that way. You looked distraught after you got that phone call this evening before I left. I thought you might need a friend."

"Roxy, that's nice of you. My parents were injured in a fire. I'm just worried about them."

"So do you want company?"

Buck paused trying to think. Roxy added, "I know you have tough manners at work, but I suspect you're really a nice guy deep down."

"Oh, OK. I can't sleep anyway. You might as well come over," Buck said and explained how to get to his apartment. After he answered the door, he watched Roxy unzip her peach sweat jacket to reveal a shirt with Tinker Bell on it. She also wore peach sweat pants. When she arrived, Buck still held the blue fleece baby blanket. He answered the unasked question.

"My mother made this for me 25 years ago. I couldn't get rid of it. She put so much work into it. I usually keep it in a drawer but decided to take it out when I couldn't sleep."

"It's pretty."

"Want some coffee?"

"Sure."

Buck draped the blanket over the couch and went into the kitchen with Roxy following. She took a seat in a chair at the table. Buck grabbed the coffee pot, put a clean filter in it and filled it with ground coffee beans and pushed the button to start brewing it. He was surprised at Roxy's question.

"Is Buck a nickname?"

"Yes. My dad gave it to me. I grew up in New York City and played with kids who lived on different floors of the apartment building. My mother, Lindsey, worked by babysitting the other children while they worked as secretaries or sales clerks. My father, Stanley, started calling me Buck because I strutted around the apartment buck naked and rode my rocking horse like a bucking bronco."

Roxy giggled. Buck took two mugs from his cabinet and filled them with the coffee.

"Do you like milk and sugar in your coffee?"

"Milk, please. Do you have vanilla?"

"Vanilla? I'll check." Buck scanned his cabinets and did not find any vanilla. "Sorry. I don't."

"It's fine. I'll just have the milk then."

Buck placed the mug in front of Roxy. He didn't know what to say next so he sat in the chair opposite her. He rubbed his hands against his robe trying to think of something, but Roxy spoke first.

"Buck, you looked so worried. Maybe, you should think about happy things."

"Like what?"

"Well, tell me about your childhood. Did you always live in

an apartment?"

At that suggestion, Buck relaxed a bit. He looked at his blanket in the living room before answering.

"Yes. My parents couldn't afford a house."

"That's sad. I like my apartment but I can't wait to have a house with a yard. Maybe when I finish school."

"Keep your dreams. My parents gave up theirs so I could get an education. Mom wanted to be a baker and Dad almost qualified for NASA's astronaut program."

"I bet your mom loved children if she babysat. Can you tell me more about her?"

"She did love children. She always wanted to open a bakery but didn't want to risk it without a business degree. Spending time with me and the other children left little time for her to go to college and study. I could count on her to bake for the church or school whenever I needed it. She also sold some of her cakes in the neighborhood. If she lives…"
At that, Buck began crying. Roxy patted his back. Buck pulled himself together and said, "I'll have her bake you one."

"That's nice. She doesn't need to go to that trouble."

"It will be my pleasure."

Roxy sipped her coffee.

"Why didn't your dad become an astronaut?"

"He never wanted to leave his job. He wanted to provide for his family. When he left the service, Mom was pregnant with me so he took the first decent job he could get. The city job was stable and had a good retirement plan. But he used to umpire our neighborhood baseball games. When he did, he told us about the different constellations in the sky and about being in the Navy. He flew planes in the Navy."

"You sound like you had a good childhood. You smiled when you were talking about your dad."

"I loved my childhood. We were so happy even though we were poor. Dad always joked about his job but he really liked working for the New York Transit Authority. We always had food on our table even if the meals were modest. Mom put any extra money into a 'college fund' bank on the shelf. I can remember many times I tried to raid that bank for candy or toys, but Mom always caught me. She slapped my wrist and said, 'Don't go blowing your college money. You must make something of yourself.'"

That memory made Buck laugh.

"Well, you're manager now. That's somethin' ain't it?" She blew a bubble.

"Yes. Mom and Dad were so proud of me when I started at the University of Virginia. When they drove me there in my freshman year and hauled my stuff into my dorm room for the first time, Mom cried for joy."

Buck's eyes began watering. Roxy grabbed a tissue from the counter and handed it to Buck. He blew his nose.

"I don't know what I will do if something happens to them. I don't speak to my friends from college much. Mom and Dad are all I have."

"Buck, I'm sure everything will be OK." She held his hand and smiled at him. She also yawned.

"Thanks Roxy. I'm glad you came over. I feel a little better now. You should go because it's really late. Can you get home safely?"

"No problem. Don't worry 'bout me." She blew another bubble.

"Good. By the way, I will be in work a little late tomorrow. I have to see my parents before work."

"I'll take care of things till you get there. Ba-Bye."

Buck walked Roxy to his door. When she left, Buck went to his bedroom again and took off his bathrobe. He threw it on the edge of the bed, slid back under the covers and fell asleep thinking of playing ball, astronauts and childhood dreams lost.


Rain pounded the window pane, and gray light filled the room, waking Buck. He sprang from his bed. He quickly showered and dressed in jeans and a polo shirt. He ate breakfast and left, catching the first El bound for the hospital.

"Can you tell me where I can find Mr. and Mrs. Robertson?" he asked the nurse on duty.

"Mrs. Robertson is in intensive care. To get to Mr. Robertson, take the hallway to the end. Turn left. First door on your right."

Thanking the nurse, he headed for his father's room. He feared the worst but was glad they were alive. He hesitated at the door. Buck tried to think of an excuse or something to say, but his mind went blank. Shaking, he walked through the door of the hospital room. He was surprised to see Angelique asleep in a chair. He looked at her briefly. One arm hung over the chair while the second was under her cheek. Her legs were curled. Her cheeks had soot on them. Although her hair had lost its shine and she had lines on her face from the chair, she maintained the same beauty he noticed the first time he met her.

The dimly lit room looked like a New York apartment only with special medical equipment. His father lay quiet and weak with bandages all over his body. A pitcher of water sat on the table by the bed. Buck had never seen his dad so still. Stanley was always moving. This fact made it harder to approach the bed. Yet he mustered as much courage as he could and walked over to him. Stanley recognized Buck and smiled a little.

"Dad? Dad?" Stanley nodded in response. "I'm sorry about last night. I wanted to come. I just couldn't. I don't even know how many visits I can make. I want to say I love you and thank you for all you've given me."

Wanting to hide his tears from his father, Buck walked into the hallway again to regain his composure. Buck thought he heard Angelique wake at the sound of his voice. He wondered what she was thinking and why she was
there. He heard a faint voice from the door say, "That's my boy."
Entering the room again, Buck took his father's hand and remained silent. He just sat there staring at Stanley. So full of life, now his spirit is being smothered. Buck glanced at Angelique watching him. She smiled at him. Buck was sure she was starting to like him. Her face nearly touched his. He could feel the tension between them. He wanted to kiss her. When the nurse came, he remembered they were in a hospital and looked away.
After an hour, he went to see his mother in intensive care. Lindsey didn't appear to be aware of anything around her. Buck couldn't stand seeing her without a bright smile. She moaned loudly, causing Buck to jump. He assumed something in her dreams was making her cry. He grabbed her hand.

"Mom, I'm here. It's me. Buck." That seemed to calm her again. He could tell she was heavily sedated. Besides the breathing apparatus, three IVs were attached to her arms and heart-monitoring equipment beeped her weak pulse.

"You must go," the nurse said.

"But…"

"She needs her rest. Go." Buck kissed his mother and glumly left the room. Angelique found him in the hallway and walked with him. The patter of rain and the humming of the instruments were all they heard. Buck was ashamed of how he must look to Angelique. His eyes were bloodshot. He hadn't bothered to comb his hair because it would take too long. His sling was dirty and stained with his mother's blood. Buck looked into Angelique's caring eyes and forced a smile.

"Thank you. You look like you spent the night here."

"I did. I didn't want your father to be alone."

"I appreciate it, but I hardly know you. Why would...?

"I know what it's like to lose parents," Angelique said as she fought the tears.

"You're parents died in a fire?"

"No."

Her expression gave away a secret that there was more to the story. Although Buck wondered about it, he respected her choice to be silent.

"Look, I hope your parents will be OK. I really need to get back to my inn and serve my guests."

Trying to sound casual but not managing it, Buck said, "I have to be at the cruise line and get back to work."

As Buck walked down the street, he could feel Angelique watching him. He didn't turn around but kept walking. Moving rapidly helped clear his head.

\* \* \*

Angelique watched him as he walked away. She felt a connection with him that she hadn't felt with any other man. Here was someone who would understand what a tragedy can do to a person. Even though Buck's parents were still alive, Angelique noticed he felt similar emotions as she felt on that night. However, she had never opened up about that night so long ago to anyone besides Maggie, and she wasn't sure she could do it even now. The memories were too painful. The rising water flashed in her mind. She saw the head bobbing in the water. She remembered the hospital staff racing to revive her father. Angelique closed her mind again. She decided she wouldn't tell Buck because she didn't want to relive that pain.

# Chapter 6
## *The Strangers on the Street*

Back at the inn, Angelique wanted to forget about the previous day. Too many things happened in 24 hours, but she couldn't shake the emotions she felt. She still was upset when she met Maggie in the dining room.

"What's wrong?" Maggie asked.

"I don't know. I think I'm just tired. Yesterday was horrifying."

"Yeah, it was. You did a good thing. Right now, you just need a hot bath and rest."

"I do. But I can't sleep."

"Why?" Maggie folded a napkin and placed it near the basket of muffins.

"That guy I told you about finally showed up this morning at the hospital. I was mad at him in the afternoon, furious with him last night, sympathetic this morning and now confused about him."

"What happened?"

Angelique walked over and grabbed a muffin from the basket.

"He broke his arm. I tried to help. Then he accused me of costing him business."

"Yeah? What else?"

"That was in the afternoon. I already told you about the phone call." Angelique chewed a blueberry.

"You did. What happened in the hospital?"

"Well, we were sitting in Mr. Robertson's room and…"

"And, what?" Maggie looked at her curiously.

"I wanted to kiss him," she blurted. "What's wrong with me? I can't stand that he works on the river and is only after money. Yet, I can't seem to keep my mind off him."

"Nothin's wrong. You just care for 'im."

"No, I don't. I couldn't. Oh, I just don't know."

Angelique broke into sobs. Maggie held her hand.

"Is this about 'im or somethin' else?"

"Of course it's about him."

"I just don' think you'd be crying if it was just 'im."

Angelique didn't want to admit that Maggie was right. She wasn't crying over Buck. She might have cried a little over him, but she really cried because she was confused over her feelings for him and her guilt. Seeing Mr. Robertson in the hospital brought back those guilty feelings that she could have done something to save her parents. *If only my father had listened to me and did not go to work that day when he was called.*

*"I have to do my duty, Doll. You understand, dontcha?"*

As if reading her thoughts, Maggie said, "It was a long time ago. Put the incident behind ya. They loved ya and were grateful for all ya tried to do."

Angelique dabbed a napkin on her face to dry her tears. Her parents did die so long ago. It still seemed like yesterday, however. Maggie changed the subject.

"Sad. So Sad," Maggie sighed. "All them people hurt. Some died. The news is sayin' arson."

"Arson? But why?"

"Don' know. They're investigatin'."

"Hmm. Maggie, how many guests do we have?"
"We have a full house, Miss. You told me to tell the firefighters that the people could stay here if they had no family. There were lot of 'em. One has a sister, but she has no room in her apartment."

"A full house for free? Oh my. What am I going to do?"
"They're not all free. Some insisted on payin'. Some are waitin' on insurance."

"Still, how am I going to stay afloat with all those free guests?"

"We'll manage. You doin' the Lord's work, offering a home to the homeless."

"Yes, but we're so financially strapped."

"Don' worry."

When Maggie left, Angelique walked up stairs to take that

much-needed hot bath. She dressed in a spring linen suit. The bright lavender and peach colors in her outfit highlighted her shiny black hair. She styled her hair into a bun and wore a clip with a bow and feathers in the back. The rose returned to her cheeks. Even though she was exhausted, she didn't want to sleep. She had work to do. Angelique closed the bedroom door behind her and walked down the stairs. The wet weather sent a chill through her body as Angelique greeted her guests. After talking to them for several minutes, she headed for her office.

Despite the rain, Angelique cracked her window in her office. She needed air. She spied two strange men arguing about something. The first one was short with a baseball cap on his head. His grungy clothes needed a good washing and one knee had a bright red patch over the brown cotton trousers. The second figure was much taller, wearing all black. His hat cast shadows on his face, but Angelique thought she knew him. He gave her an eerie feeling that turned her skin to ice. Bits of the conversation drifted through the window.

"Where are they? You promised them by now," the tall man demanded.

"You'll get yours…need more time," the short man pleaded.

"No more time. Tonight."

"Your manager is suspicious already."
"Don't worry about him. You'll get them to me tonight or the Feds find out about what happened down the street."

He pointed at something that Angelique couldn't see. The conversation did not make much sense, but it disturbed her. As she thought about what she had heard, the taller figure noticed her looking out the window. She suspected the taller figure knew that she had heard the conversation.

He said, "Let's get out of here. People might see us."

Both men left in opposite directions. Angelique was curious

and decided to see if she could find out more. She left the inn and crossed the street at the same time the taller figure crossed. Recognizing Mr. Kennedy, she shivered. She decided she had made a mistake and was about to go back to the inn when he blocked her path.

"Excuse me, I would like to pass."

He grinned and didn't budge. "Such a pretty."

"Thank you." Angelique felt ice return to her skin and it had nothing to do with the wind and rain.

"Where you headed?"

"I was taking a walk. I…I like rain." Taking a breath and reinstating her resolve, she said, "Besides, I don't have to tell you where I'm going. It's none of your business. Let me pass."

"Why?" He grabbed her arm. "You going to the police?"

"What on earth for? Let me go!"

"To report what you might have seen."
"All I saw was two men arguing. That is hardly illegal. Let me GO!" Angelique trembled in his grip. She tried to retain composure.
He released his hold but still would not let her pass. Angelique shook uncontrollably.

"You better not be lying, Miss Chalfonte."

Angelique didn't like the threatening look of his eyes. "I'm not."

"Good," he sneered. He licked his lips.

"Yet, you still won't let me pass!"

"All right, Pretty. You are free." Mr. Kennedy said and stepped aside. Her fear made Kennedy smile. Angelique wondered if he liked women he could control. She did not look back. Although he said she was free, she knew she wasn't. Mr. Kennedy was bound to do something about this. She didn't want to go back to the inn when she was afraid. She needed to go somewhere where she would feel safe and relax. Not even flinching, she took off for the pier. She knocked on Buck's door.

"Buck?"

"Come in."

"Angelique. What a surprise. I thought you had to be at the inn." Her hands trembled and she was breathing very fast.

"What's wrong?"

"I was at the inn. I saw…"

She remembered Kennedy's warning.
She said, "I must have gotten in Mr. Kennedy's way. I couldn't cross the street."

"Why would you be this scared?"

"He got mad at me. He grabbed my arm. I'm fine, though. I don't know why I'm bothering you with this, especially when you have work to do."

She saw the mounds of paperwork on his desk

"Coming here just felt right, but I'll go."

"Relax. I'm glad you came." He opened his arm without the sling. She ran to him and let those strong biceps wrap her shaking body. Suddenly, her body stopped shaking. It was as if the world disappeared while he held her. Buck's warmth lit a fire in her heart that spread to her toes.

"So, what happened?" he asked.

"Nothing. He finally let me go. I ran all the way here. I don't think he followed me."

"You can't stay here. He'll fire me for sure. Besides, he owns the cruise line and could be here at any time."

"There are more important things than a job."

"I need this job. I can't explain it. You have to trust me."

"Trust you? You put money over everything."

"No I don't." He looked angrily at her.

"Can't you get another job?"

"I need this one. I can't talk about this, just now." Angelique saw Buck's expression change to one of concern. "Are you all right?"

"My arm hurts a little, but I think I'll be all right. I should get back to the inn, but I just don't want to be around people right now. My inn is crowded with retirees."

"Why don't we go out to the dock? At least, I'll still be working. Do you know any French? You can help with the Canadian tourists."

"OK. Yes, but I'm not very good. My parents wanted to forget their homeland. Then, they died in my teens. So I didn't pick up much."

"Mind the rain?"

"No. Buck, thank you for your help." She still was confused about him. Sometimes, he valued his job and supported Kennedy.

Other times, he offered a hand to help as if he genuinely cared for her.

"No problem."

The wind from the river ripped through their clothes. The rain hit their coats hard. Angelique wandered along the pier watching Buck inspect his ships. She got a sick feeling when she looked at the river in the rain. She could see the Coast Guard ship swaying on the high water. She wanted to scream to her dad and tell him to watch those waves. She wanted to tell her mother to stay at the inn. But she couldn't. Looking at Buck, she thought about his occupation again. She didn't like that he worked with ships. She didn't like being this close to the river. Buck's job, the weather, the river and her memories were making her dizzy. The temperature in her cheeks was increasing. She put her hands to her cheeks to cool them.

"Why was Mr. Kennedy so mean to you? Does it have to do with the letter?"

Startled, she said, "What? No."

"Then what could possibly make Mr. Kennedy keep you from crossing a street?"

"Uh. I don't know." She didn't like where this conversation was heading.

"Do you think he'll come after you again?"

"I don't think so," she lied. It must have shown on her face.

"Are you sure?"

"Yes, I'm sure. You know what? I think you're right. I better go." She fled back to the inn.

*** 

Buck stood at the dock where she left puzzled. He couldn't understand her. Sometimes, she wanted his help. Other times, she got angry or was mysterious. He knew she was lying about Kennedy but didn't know why. He shrugged and went back to his work. After leaving the dock, he reflected on Angelique's visit in his office. Before she came he was having a gloomy day. He was glad she came even if her visit was mysterious. The visit to his parents drained him emotionally.

Buck went back to his accounting work. No matter what he did, he couldn't get the numbers to balance. There definitely was money missing. He checked and rechecked. He also couldn't stop thinking about Angelique. He knew she hadn't told him everything about what happened between her and Mr. Kennedy and was concerned for her safety. *I wonder if he threatened her in some way. He better not have because I will kill him if he hurts her.*

# Chapter 7
## *The Private Voyage*

Buck continued writing his letter to executives of local companies. He needed new referrals, and another day of rain meant more problems for the cruise line. Some workers arrived late, and he recorded their names. Even though he knew the weather had something to do with it, Buck decided to dock their pay to appease Mr. Kennedy but not the full amount. He probably would have to fire some of them if they continued to show up late to work. Roxy came over to Buck.

"Buck, sir, the 4 o'clock trip is overbooked because I have to close the top deck again. What should I do?"

"Don't refund them. Move them to the 8 o'clock trip."

"Can't. The 8 o'clock was canceled."

"Canceled?"

"By Mr. Kennedy. He needs the ship for a private affair tonight. He came in before you and told me."

Buck frowned. "Is he getting the private affair rate for that?"

"No one gave *me* any money."

"That doesn't make sense. He would want the profits."

"Maybe he was given the money directly."

"That could be."

"It's his boat, you know," Roxy said.

"Yeah. It just sounds weird. He knows that all bookings go through you and you get the money."

Roxy shrugged.

"I don't know about it. I only know what he told me."

Buck let it go. Roxy was right. He was entitled to use he ships for private trips if he wanted.

"OK. Put the extra people from the 4 o'clock on tomorrow's 10 o'clock."

"What if they can't make tomorrow?"

"So be it. Make it their choice. Our policy is we don't give refunds."

"We shouldn't do that. That would be cheating people."

"I don't cheat people. I'm still willing to give them their paid three-hour tour. It's not my fault if they can't make it."

"Still, it sounds cold."

Buck was frustrated. He liked Roxy. She helped him when he needed a friend, but he had a job to do.

"Roxy, I'm the manager. You have no say in how I run the business. Now go."

"Yes, Sir."

Roxy went back to the ticket counter clearly upset. Buck peeked out his door at her. He didn't like being so mean to her. He saw her doodling and imagined they were insults about him. He sighed and closed the door. Alone in his office, Buck contemplated the private voyage. The cruise line often rented the ship for weddings and parties, but they usually took place on a weekend. This was a Wednesday, and it was raining. Private parties do not want to be on the river in the rain. And it looked like Mr. Kennedy wasn't getting paid for the private voyage. Buck's mind buzzed with all the questions he had
about Mr. Kennedy. He wanted answers to so many questions. He decided to search the touring company building after hours.

❧ ❧ ❧

Angelique sat by her bedroom window. She thought about everything that happened that day. She did not know why Mr. Kennedy grabbed her. She knew that it had something to do with what she heard. She knew the topic had to be about something illegal despite what she told Mr. Kennedy. Otherwise, he would not have been so concerned that she would go to the police. But she didn't know what she could tell the authorities. She had heard two men arguing. It could have been about anything. She decided against telling Buck because of Kennedy's warning and because she did not trust Buck. He could be part of the illegal activities. He has been causing her problems.

Angelique hoped she did not give away her secret to Buck who she thought was suspicious of what happened. Still, Angelique wondered what Kennedy was doing. She shook her head. Her memory of Kennedy's cold, threatening eyes made her vow to stay away from Buck and the Delaware River Touring Co. She was safer that way.

# Chapter 8
## *Angelique's Fears*

Two weeks passed. Angelique did not go near the dock or the river. When she was not serving guests, she sat in her bedroom or office. She avoided conversations with Maggie as well because she didn't want Maggie to be worried. She kept busy trying to deal with the diminishing finances of her inn. Despite having a full house, she struggled to make ends meet. She wondered if Buck cared about what she was doing. He probably had forgotten about her and moved onto someone else because she had acted so strangely the last time she saw him. A man that handsome would have his pick of women. *He certainly flirted with my guests during my reception.*

Angelique moved from her bed to the desk. She thought maybe she would write him a letter. Mr. Kennedy would not see it, but she remembered she didn't know where Buck lived, only where he worked. She didn't want to send a letter to his office. Angelique also seemed to be at a loss for words. Each time she started to write, she ripped the rose-embossed stationery. Her room quickly filled with torn sheets of paper. She could not tell Buck what she overheard and that he might be involved with something illegal. Plus she had other worries to address. Truth was she missed him. She's not sure why she missed him. He laughed at her, caused her to lose revenues and might be part of something illegal. He put people at risk daily and didn't care. He must be Mr. Kennedy's right-hand man.

Angelique sighed. She walked over to her bed, plopped on

the comforter and stared at the ceiling. So many little things about the Delaware River Touring Co. made her mad. She hated the way Mr. Kennedy took the ships out in all weather despite the dangers. She hated that Buck treated his customers and employees horribly. She was right to stay away from the place. Still, something about the company and its manager controlled her heart. Sighing again, Angelique stood and left her bedroom.

On the second landing, Angelique bumped into Mrs. O'Reilly, a plump woman with sandy-gray hair. She was one of the fire victims.

"Sorry, Mrs. O'Reilly."

"You'd do well to watch where you're going."

Angelique said, "I guess I'm just distracted today."

Mrs. O'Reilly put her finger to her forehead. "Do you need to talk about it?"

"I don't want to trouble you."

"Honey, listen. The guests are chatting away downstairs about politics and I don't much care for that. I was going to my room, but I'd rather have company."

Angelique hesitated. She wanted to talk to someone about her feelings and her fears. She wanted someone to tell her she wasn't crazy, which is what Maggie had said for years.

"You know, I think I'll take you up on your offer."

"Splendid."

Mrs. O'Reilly unlocked her door and motioned Angelique to enter. Angelique smiled as she looked at Mrs. O'Reilly's pictures.

"That's my sister. These five pictures are all that survived the fire."

"Sorry to hear that."

"At least I have some of my mementos here, but I'm sad. I can't wait to go back."

Angelique walked to the bed and sat on a puffy pillow with lace trim.

"Aren't you afraid to go back?"

"Honey, your inn is nice, but I want to be in my own surroundings again. And I can't do anything about what happened so there's no point in brooding over it."

"Yes but a tragedy like that has to have affected you."

Mrs. O'Reilly thought about that.

"I want the person responsible to pay, but no, I'm not afraid. Why do you ask?"

"It brought back memories."

"Do you mean your fear of the river?"

Angelique looked at Mrs. O'Reilly questioningly.

"Maggie noticed that you've been hiding and is worried about you. She mentioned how much you don't like the river. She believes you have been hiding because of something that happened on the river."

"Not really, but it's related. I wasn't always like this."

"Like what?"

"Afraid and hostile toward the river."

"What changed you?" Mrs. O'Reilly asked.

"The river excited me when I was young. I would go to Penns' Landing as a little girl and would watch the water traffic. One day, my mom and I fought. I ran out the house and ran to the river. I saw a child needing help. My mother caught up with me a short while later. I tried to tell my mother about the child needing help, but she thought I was making it up. She didn't see anyone. I tried to plead with her, but she was mad that I had run off by myself."

Intrigued, Mrs. O'Reilly said, "What happened?"

"Before my mother got there, he called out, 'Help me, please.' But I couldn't help him because I was alone. When my mother came, she pulled me away too fast. She said, 'Angel, let's go. You're in trouble for running away'. I tried to show her the boy, but she didn't believe me. He had disappeared."

"What happened to the boy?"

"I don't know. I'm afraid he died and that it was my fault. I never told my mother about these guilty feelings. After that, I hated water."

"Maggie said something about your parents."

"Well Maggie didn't know about the earlier incident. The accident of my father was the second time the river failed me."

Mrs. O'Reilly opened a drawer and pulled out a blanket. "Are you cold?"

"No. I'm fine."

Mrs. O'Reilly sat on the bed and put the blanket over her legs.

"Go on."

"A nor'easter raged up and down the East Coast. Piles of snow melted and flooded the streets. The rain raised water levels in the river. My father was in the Coast Guard at the time and called to rescue stranded residents. One family was caught in the swollen river."

"When was this?"

"I was 14, so, about seven years ago."

"Hmmm. My daughter, her husband and my granddaughter were caught in that flood."

Angelique was surprised at how small the world was. Here was a member of the family her father tried to help. Now she was doing the same thing.

"Well my mom was on the side of the bank, volunteering to help with sandbags. I was back at the inn watching the rescue on the news with Maggie's mother and Maggie. Mom saw a huge wave coming and called to my dad to watch out. But Dad couldn't hear her. He was knocked overboard. Mom stood in the rain, freezing and calling to him and wouldn't leave until she knew he was safe despite the advice of the rescue personnel. Eventually, the team saw a bobbing head and brought a man to safety. My mother saw it was my father and took the advice of the police to meet him at the hospital."

Angelique became pale.

"Are you all right, Honey?"

"I'm fine. These memories are hard to handle. That's why I try to bury them and move on with my life," Angelique said.

"But it's obvious that you can't keep these bottled up. It's making you sick. And it's keeping you from experiencing life. You're too afraid and angry."

"I know."

"So what happened to them?" Mrs. O'Reilly asked.

"Well my dad was pronounced dead at the hospital. My mom caught pneumonia and died a few weeks later."

"I'm so sorry to hear about your parents. It must have been hard for you after that."

"Thanks, Mrs. O'Reilly. It was. Maggie's mother was a great comfort. She was my guardian until I turned 18. I had no one else. I have aunts and uncles in France, but no one in America. My grandmother came here when Dad was three. My grandfather had just died. Grand-mère wanted a new life. She died before I was born. Mom's family remain in France. She met Dad in college and got married. They bought this inn. This is all I have known. I never met my French relatives although I have written to them."

Angelique paused, thinking about Buck.

"Is there something more?"

"I just don't know how to discuss these feelings with people who love the water."

Mrs. O'Reilly smiled.

"You're young. You'll figure it out when you need to open up to the man you love. Besides, you told me."

Angelique nodded.

"You're the first person I've told since Maggie. But I don't think I want to tell anyone else."

"Then don't. But you have to let go of your anger somehow."

Angelique agreed. She suddenly was worried about Buck. She wanted to confide in Mrs. O'Reilly about the secret she had.

"There's something else that happened. I'm worried about something I overheard."

"Is it about you or your business?"

"No."

"Then, you have no worries. The information is someone else's business. Don't go poking your nose in other people's business if you can avoid it."

"But someone might be in danger or worse doing something he shouldn't be."

"Honey, listen. If what you heard is dangerous, then you'll be putting yourself at risk. If it's illegal, the police will eventually catch it. That's their job. Yours is to run an inn."

"Thanks, Mrs. O'Reilly. That puts things into perspective for me."

Angelique decided to get some tea and cookies and went down stairs only to be stopped by Maggie.

"Ya been hidin' lately."

"I had things on my mind."

"Things? Ya mean a certain gentleman."

"No. I've been worried about the finances. Buck means nothing to me. I have been tired from the hard work," Angelique said.

"Why use his name if he means nothin'?" Maggie asked.

"I don't know."

"No need to lie to me, Miss. Ya won't gain nothin'."

"OK. So what if I had him on my mind?" Angelique looked annoyed.

"Ya ought to know yer feelings or you'll never get no rest. Mom always said."

"I know my feelings. I don't want to go near that business again." Angelique scowled.

"Ya sound angry," said Maggie, concerned.

"Not really." Angelique brightened.

"Well, anger will hurt yer heart. I let go of mine."

"What anger?" she asked curiously.

"Anger at Mom for taking a lowly position. Mom was smart! She could have been something important, but she worked for yer parents as a nanny and tutor. Long ago, when we became friends, I forgave her."

"Your mother always told me how much she loved living with my parents. She told me she never wanted to teach in a school because of the kids who never did any work. She loved being around people at the inn. She taught them about the history of the city. It gave her joy."

"I never knew that," Maggie said surprised.

"And what about you? You were finished with the Philadelphia City College. You had an offer to work at one of the upscale hotels as a housekeeping manager, but you came back here to help your mother even though I couldn't pay as much."

"Miss Angelique, you're me friend. You needed me. Mom's health was failing. She needed me too. You're the one who said there are more important things than a job."

"Yeah. I know. Thanks for staying." She hugged Maggie.

# Chapter 9
## *Trouble at the Pier*

Buck didn't realize that two weeks had passed since he last saw Angelique. He had been so busy at work that nothing else mattered. It rained nine of the 14 days. Also in those two weeks, trips were canceled. Passengers were moved to different cruises. Employees were fired, and he noticed a steady drop in tourists' bookings as a result of Angelique's not recommending the tours.

He was unable to find a replacement inn. The large hotels wanted payment to advertise in their lobby brochure boxes. Other bed and breakfasts didn't have the reputation the 1776 Inn had. He now understood why Kennedy wanted Angelique's recommendations. He had at least put some brochures at the Philadelphia Convention and Visitor's Bureau. He also got a small motel on Spruce Street to recommend his touring company. That motel was not going to replace the revenue lost from the 1776 Inn. Besides all these problems, Buck continued to notice strange behavior among crew members. He hadn't had time to investigate the crew. Mr. Kennedy wouldn't appreciate the losses. He still didn't know where the original money went. The business was failing under his management. He didn't know what to do.

But Buck had been lucky that Mr. Kennedy hadn't checked on the business for a long time. While he relished the time away from Kennedy, he wondered where Kennedy was and what he was doing. Buck had other more pressing matters.
Throughout these difficult times, Buck longed to see Angelique's beautiful smile. She could always cheer him even

on days when he had so many problems. Buck ached to hold her, especially now that his arm had healed. Her soft rosy skin would definitely brighten his otherwise dreary days. However, he didn't have time to contact her or leave his office. So he ignored his desires for her and focused on running the touring company.

The door swung open. Buck hoped it was Angelique, but Mr Kennedy stood in the door way. *Damn!*

"Mr. Robertson, explain these losses!"

"Sir, you canceled several trips and the ships needed repair or you could have been sued. I have tried to double trips to regain some of the lost profit, but I also need new workers."

"I see. At least you've taken the right approach. You want workers, go to the job training facilities. Immigrants would be more than happy to work here."

"Yes sir. I guess I can look into that. I wanted to talk to you about something else."

"What?"

"Well, about this missing money…"

"What missing money? I did those books myself before you came. I didn't notice anything out of the ordinary."

Buck was concerned. "I've done the accounts several times. I can't get the numbers to add up. Do you know what happened to the money?"

"You're the manager. You're supposed to know where my money is going."

Buck stood his ground. He didn't like Kennedy's tone. "Sir, you don't think that I…"

"You? Ha! You aren't smart enough to take company money."

This surprised Buck, but he let Kennedy think it passed without his noticing. The words of the article on embezzling came back to him as Mr. Kennedy left. Now he was faced with a new problem—the hiring of new workers. Buck didn't like the idea of hiring immigrants. That could put Delaware River Touring Co. at risk. Besides, they did not speak English, but he had no choice. He needed workers that would accept cheap wages. College students and recent graduates usually wanted more money.

Buck walked over to an apartment complex near his parents' retirement facility. It had a job center in the main office. Gray clouds hung over the water and city, worsening his already gloomy mood. He hadn't been in that part of town since the fire. His parents remained in the hospital. Stanley appeared to be growing stronger, but Lindsey took a turn for the worse. Doctors said any day now. Buck knew his mother was a fighter. "Any day now" could mean months with Lindsey. A queasy feeling hit his stomach hard. He was about to enlist workers into hard labor with little compensation. Buck took a deep breath and opened the door that led to a courtyard in front of the main office. Workers were gathered and talking about whatever occupied their minds. When Buck entered the office, he was met by a woman who was talking about grown children to a colleague.

She said, "What do you want Fancy Pants?"

"Hello, Mrs. Mateo. How are you?"

"Em all right. You? Word on the street is your parents were in that fire. My sister also got it."

Buck nodded. "My parents are in the hospital, Mrs. Mateo. Dad is getting better. I don't know what will happen to Mom, but I've come for another reason."

"Yeah?"

"You see," Buck said to the plump woman with the silver curls who wore a dress with flowers on the pattern. Mrs. Mateo leaned over the chair so she could hear better. "I am manager of Delaware River Touring Company. I need workers."

"Yeah? A manager. Lindsey and Stanley must be so proud!"

"Yes, Mrs. Mateo. Know anyone looking for work?" I can pay $100 per week."

"Well, now. I'll ask around. Anyone interested, where should I send 'em?"

"The dock at pier 10. There is a small ticket office. My office is off to the right. OK?"

"Some of our friends don't speak English. They can't read neither."

"Well, in that case, tell them to look for a small office on the pier. The ticket counter worker can speak Spanish. When they come, tell them to say the word, 'work' and I'll understand."

"OK. Now, sit a spell and I'll tell ya all the gossip."

"Mrs. Mateo, I have to get back to work."

"Nonsense. My little Buckie boy has time for his mother's best friend."

Buck had to stay or he would be branded a snob. Buck remembered Lindsey met Mrs. Mateo when she moved into the retirement community. They had known each other for only five years, but she always acted like she knew them all his life. Buck visited with Mrs. Mateo occasionally when he saw his parents. So he sat and listened. He enjoyed hearing the news. It took his mind off other problems he was having and brightened his day. However, had he left he wouldn't have missed Angelique.

* * *

Angelique realized that the only way she could relieve her anger was to see Buck herself. She decided to stop at the dock. When she got there, Buck was gone. She started to write him a note when the door flung open. Looking up, she saw Franklin Kennedy.

"Well now. If it isn't Little Lady Chalfonte. Snooping around the manager's office are you? Trying to find out more about what you saw?"

"No, of course not."

"What are you doing here? Do you have a thing with my manager?"

Angelique remained frozen. She was unable to speak. She felt a lump enter her throat.

"You're looking mighty fine in that there business suit. You ever been with a Real man? I could teach you things that the quivering boy could never show you!"

Angelique's eyes filled with water. She was determined not to cry. She wouldn't give Mr. Kennedy the satisfaction of knowing that she was scared. *Where are you, Buck?*

"If you're wondering where your precious man is, I sent him to get workers. We're alone, my Pretty."

He rubbed her cheek. Angelique flinched. Mr. Kennedy wet his lips. Mr. Kennedy gazed up and down Angelique's body. She quickly covered herself. She didn't know what else to do. Angelique stared at Kennedy trying to figure out what he was thinking. Angelique thought he was a wolf about to pounce its prey. She managed some words.

"I better be going, then."

Teasing her, he said, "No. Stay. We could have fun."

Angelique wanted to get out of there. "What do you want?"

"With you?"

"Yes," she said, shaking.

Mr. Kennedy laughed.

"Quite a bit."

Angelique tried to act casually.

"You can keep wanting, then."

"I always get what I want, but I have something to do in the office, first."

"Does it have something to do with that conversation from a couple of weeks ago?" She blurted out the question and regretted it immediately. This changed Kennedy's tone.

Mr. Kennedy grabbed her arm. "I knew you were snooping. The less you know the better, my Sweet."

He pulled her tighter.

"You saw nothing that day, got it?"

"Yes. Yes," she sobbed.

Mr. Kennedy let her go.

When she regained some composure, she said, "I'll be leaving you to your business now."

"No, my Prissy. You're not going anywhere." Mr. Kennedy

took her into his arms and crushed her back. He wet his lips again. He pushed her against the window. Holding Angelique with one hand, he move the second one down her suit. Mr. Kennedy felt the full breast under his touch and tried to kiss her. She moved her head away. He slapped her. The tears began again.

"Stop crying, you bitch!" Angelique couldn't stop. "You give me one kiss and you're gone." He squeezed her breast harder. Then, he moved his hand lower. Mr. Kennedy grabbed her face to kiss her again. Terrified, she faced him. He planted his mouth on hers. She felt bitterness, anger and hatred in the sloppy wet kiss. When he pulled his mouth off hers, she spit in his face.

"You Bastard! Let me go!"

"As promised."

He released her not before getting a last touch with his hands. Just then, Buck entered the office.

"What's going on here?"

"Nothing. Just giving the lovely Miss Chalfonte a tour of the place."

Buck stared at Angelique. She tried to hide the terror and tears in her eyes.

"Angelique?"

"Nothing. I'm fine."

Mr. Kennedy stormed from the office looking at his watch. Still not sure whether she could trust him, Angelique vowed to herself not to tell Buck what happened even though he looked doubtful.

"Are you all right?" Buck asked with his arms open.

"Yes," she answered with a high-pitched voice and trembling hands.

"So what are you doing here?" Buck changed the subject to ease the tension in the room.

"I came to see you. I want to apologize for avoiding you for two weeks."

"Two weeks? Has it been that long? I've been so busy that I didn't notice."

She ran into his arms. The strong biceps felt like a blessing after the harsh ones of Mr. Kennedy.

"What was Kennedy doing here? I just saw him this morning."

"I don't know. I don't think he expected me to be here."

"Hmmm. Well, you're safe now." Buck rubbed Angelique's arms. She felt that familiar tingle again. The same one she felt in the hospital. Her heart wanted Angelique to keep seeing Buck. Her fear over his job would keep her head from listening to her heart. It told her to stay away. But no other man has made her feel this way. She saw excitement in Buck's eyes. She wondered if he was happy he was holding her. She also saw mystery in them and a conscious effort to hide something.

"I better go," she said and left.

# Chapter 10
## *The Death*

Several hours later, Buck heard pounding on the door. He decided Kennedy couldn't be at the door and that Angelique had guests at the inn. Buck hesitated.

"Who's there?"

"Work," was all he heard as a response. Buck opened the door.

Eleven young men and women stood there. Buck guessed these people were sent by Mrs. Mateo.

"Roxy, come into the office," Buck said.

"Okie-dokie."

To Roxy, he said, "I need you to translate."
Then to the workers, he said, "Are you here for the workers' positions?"

All 11 responded yes. Buck hired them without the formality of paperwork. It would take too long to explain it to them. Buck talked to the group.

"My name is Buck Robertson. Two doors down, you'll find a closet with blue and white-striped uniforms. You'll each need two sets. We take the cost of the uniforms out of your pay. If you are late to work, your pay is docked. If you're ill and you take off, you don't paid for that day. If you don't show for two days, you're fired." *God I hate that part. That damn Kennedy!* "We have tourists coming in an hour. Any problems you have, you can come to me. I will try to answer them as best I can. This is dangerous work. If you don't report for the first assignment, I will take that to mean you don't want the job. Any questions?"

Roxy explained that everyone understood the conditions. No one had any questions or problems. "We have two shifts, 8 to 4:30 and 3:30 to 12. Meals are unpaid." Buck picked two people as foremen for each shift and divided the rest into shifts. "Roxy will book the tourists. You can ask her questions."

Roxy handed out the garments. They quickly donned their uniforms. The morning shifts only had to work a few hours before they could leave. The rest headed for the boats for the afternoon and evening cruises. The workers learned as they went. Some of the more experienced ones helped the new people. They had to clean the boats, fill the cafes with food, empty the trash, greet the tourists, help them on the ships and cast off. The new workers relieved some of Buck's tension. Now, he could run the company for several more months to regain some of the lost revenue. He still didn't know what to do about missing cash. *I know it couldn't be any of them. None of them look smart enough. The article said…* His train of thought vanished. He had to find time to search lockers.
When the tourists entered at 3:45 p.m. for the 4 o'clock sail, all the new workers appeared ready to serve them. Because he could let the workers handle the tourists for a change and because he had gotten caught up on his work this morning, Buck had a golden opportunity to search the lockers of the older workers. He didn't know what he would find. The money disappeared months ago. However, Buck took his master keys to open the first locker, that of Ritchie Dublin. Inside, he saw the second uniform and a luggage bag. Unzipping the bag, Buck found several files taken from his

office. *Why steal the files?* Buck took the files. The rest of the locker had socks, letters from family members and books on how to become an American citizen. No money.

Buck relocked the locker and opened Enrique Bañal's. Again, Buck found another uniform, socks, letters and education manuals. He also saw a manuscript titled, *The Smuggler's Secret. A writer?* Buck jumped when he peeked behind the manuscript. A gun! *Why does he have a gun?* Buck put everything back into place and relocked the locker. He made a note to himself to find out if the gun was registered. He doubted it. He headed back to his office. Roxy had tacked a note to his door. Ripping the note from the door, Buck entered his office. He sat at his desk and found a knife to open the letter.

"Dear Mr. Robertson:

We regret to inform you that your mother, Lindsey Robertson, has passed away. Please claim the body and collect her belongings. Cause of death was complications to her burn wounds. Have a nice day.

Sincerely,
Thomas Jefferson University Hospital staff."

Buck burst into tears. He couldn't remember when he last saw Lindsey. He couldn't get away from the office much. "I think it was Tuesday. I tried to get her to smile," Buck said out loud as if someone else was in the room. *God, she didn't even die smiling. That was not like her. She was always happy.*

"I have to get to the hospital," Buck told Roxy and showed her the note.

Riding the El, Buck tried to think of something to say to his father and just stared into space, unbelieving that this tragedy occurred. He hoped that the hospital staff didn't tell his father. They were so cold about the death. *Lindsey was not a human being to them. She was just another patient.* He didn't notice the other riders.

As far as he was concerned, he rode the train alone. The driver announced the arrival of the hospital station. Buck left. He forced his legs to climb the few stairs to the entrance. Aimlessly, he showed the letter to the receptionist. She guided Buck down the basement to the morgue and introduced him to the director of the morgue.

"Right, Mr. Robertson. You will find your mother over here in the corner. Next to the body, you will see a box of her things. Would you like us to call an undertaker for you?"

Hesitating to look, Buck squinted at the body and nodded to the morgue director. "I would—appreciate—any help." He gulped.

"Fine. We have a very good one that deals with this hospital a lot. I'll ring him for you."

"She's not smiling. She should be smiling," Buck said. He began shaking.

"What did you say?"

"My father. What about my father? She's sad."

"We didn't inform your father. We thought that given his condition, you would prefer to tell him."

"Yes." Buck's breathing became short and shallow. His face drained of color. "I have to know she's happy."

"Mr. Robertson, you should calm down. Please, go out into the hall. There's a seat for you. You can get some air."

Buck didn't move. He remained mesmerized by the body.

The morgue director asked his assistant to guide him to the hall. The assistant held Buck's hand until feeling returned to his limbs. Soon, Buck's face turned a faint pink. He remembered when Brady, his pet beagle died. The dog had chased a cat across the street. The driver of the car couldn't stop before hitting Brady. He died at the pet hospital later. Lindsey comforted Buck.

"Buck, Brady will be protected by St. Francis."

"Are you sure?" he said to his mother.

She nodded and held his hand. As a child, he couldn't understand what had happened to his dog.

He said to his mother, "How could God take away something I love?"

She said, "Everything must die. God will heal those who are sad in time."

Eventually, Buck felt better about his dog's death. Now, sitting outside the morgue, he felt 10 times worse than he felt when his dog died. *Who is going to comfort me now?*

"Are you all right, Mr. Robertson?"

"I think I'm OK. I'm just shocked, I guess."

"You're not the first. It's hard. Don't worry about a thing. The hospital will take care of all the details. Go see your father."

"I'll do that."

Buck climbed the stairs to his father's room. His father sat in the bed worried about Lindsey. Buck dreaded this moment and stood in the door way. He moved aside as a floor nurse left the room. She told him she had to leave to deliver her sister's baby. He remained in the doorway. He couldn't move. As he looked down the hall, a figure carrying flowers was emerging. Buck's heart leaped as she got closer. Angelique approached the room. He could feel the sweat dripping from his hands. He rubbed them on his pants.

"Angelique, why are you here?"

"My guests like to dine at one of Philadelphia's restaurants for dinner, so I usually have some free time. I have been bringing flowers every day to your father. I told him that some were for your mother but I can't visit her as she's in ICU. I like to keep him company. He and I talk."

He turned his blood-shot eyes away before saying, "That's nice."

"Buck, what's wrong?"

"I have to tell my father."

"You have to tell your father what?"

Angelique gave Buck a burst of courage. He could accomplish any task with her by his side. He believed she would be the comfort he needed. He spoke incoherently.

"You know, it's funny."

"What's funny?"

"The circle of life. Someone dies. Someone is born. That's just the way it is."

Angelique did not understand what Buck said.

"Buck, are you all right? You don't make much sense."

"My mother died."

"I'm so sorry. Take my arm. We'll tell him together."

He entwined his arm in Angelique's. He looked at her hazel eyes bursting with compassion and sorrow. Her smile melted his fears. He saw love dancing in her look. He noticed how her skin sparkled against the dimly lit room. She was the light of the room.

"Buck, glad you're here. They won't tell me about Lindsey."

"I know, Dad." Stanley smiled at Angelique.

"I'm glad you're here too. I enjoy our talks." Angelique smiled.

Buck watched his father look at Angelique. It reminded him of the way Stanley felt about Lindsey. However, Buck saw a difference. Stanley treated Angelique like a daughter instead of a wife.

"So, Son. About your mother…"

"Dad, this is so hard for me to say."

"It's OK. Just tell me."

"Mom has uh." Buck turned away crying.

"Mr. Robertson, what Buck is trying to tell you is that your wife has passed away due to complications of her injuries. We're so sorry." To Buck, she said, "I'll leave you alone now."

"No. Please stay," both men pleaded together.

"Are you sure?"

"Yes. You're not intruding. You're a blessing," Buck said after he rubbed away his tears.

Stanley asked, "Buck, is this true?"

"Yes, Dad. I just saw her."

"Oh God! Why her? She's so sweet and loving. She always worked for others. I won't believe she's dead!"

Buck tapped his father's shoulder. He pulled up a chair and sat near him, but he couldn't look at him. He kept his gaze on Angelique who was shivering. He could tell she was deep in thought.

"What are you thinking about?"

"I'm thinking that I know what you're going through. It was horrible when my mom died."

"You don't have to talk about it," Buck said reassuringly.

"Thanks, but I feel you need to hear it."

"I don't know. I'm not thinking about much right now. My mind's blank. I just want to be here for my father."

Buck turned toward Stanley whose heart monitor started going crazy. Stanley was silent and cold. Buck moved the blanket up to his chest. Angelique grabbed Stanley's hand and sang a little song to calm him. As she sang, Buck remembered the day they first met. He couldn't believe how beautiful she was then. Now, her singing was more pleasant than anything that Buck has heard.
He imagined an angel came down from heaven to sing to his father. Buck was comforted by her beautiful eyes, and her body excited him as she took each breath for the song. *Why does she hate what I do so much? If she only knew the truth…* When Angelique finished her song, Stanley slept. Buck smiled at Angelique. He knew he couldn't have faced this without her.

"I think I better let my father rest. Was this how it was when your mother died?"

"My mother was in the hospital barely breathing. I couldn't bear to see her that way so I decided to hang with my friends instead of going to the hospital. I was 14. No one knew how to reach me when she died. After I got home several hours later, I got the call to come to the hospital. I felt terrible that I wasn't there for Mom. I have made a point to help anyone I can ever since. I owe her that much."

"Angelique, I don't think you did anything wrong. I'm having a hard time dealing with my mom's death and I'm 25. I don't know what I would have done if I was 14."

"I wish I could convince myself of that. Maggie, my housekeeper, keeps telling me to let it go, that it happened so long ago. I just can't."

"We all grieve in our own way."

Buck wrapped his arms around her as the two left the room to let Stanley rest.

# Chapter 11
## *The Kiss*

"Do you want something to drink?" Angelique asked.

"Yes."

"I think the cafeteria is this way."

Angelique guided Buck along a corridor until they came to the hospital cafeteria, which was a large room with tables and chairs. The food service was along the wall with cash registers at the end of the service area. She admired his chest as he breathed heavily. With each breath Buck took, Angelique's heart beat faster. She knew the death had nothing to do with what she felt. She had this reaction every time she saw him. His wavy hair and those eyelashes always made her body melt. Angelique wanted to rub her fingers over his chest and feel his skin beneath her touch, but she did not dare because he had just lost his mother.

Angelique saw Buck watching her. She couldn't see what he was thinking because his face was blank. He was distraught, she decided. She smiled at him when he eyed her clothes and how they fit perfectly on her. She always liked clothes that emphasized every curve of her body. She was unaware that her pearly black hair graced her shoulder occasionally enticing Buck. Angelique felt a warmth go through her when she took Buck's hand. Buck began playing with her hair with the other. He dropped his hand.

Angelique suspected he reminded himself of where they were. She didn't want him to stop though, but she knew that she shouldn't flirt with a man who was grieving the loss of a parent even one as handsome as Buck. As she walked toward the counter, she took light steps. She felt like the floor was made of feathers.

"Here we are."

She handed him some tea and smiled. Angelique studied his face as he drank. She sipped her tea but she wanted to drink from him. She thought that his eyes wanted the same thing. Suddenly, Buck put down the cup and grabbed her. She gazed into his eyes and felt kindness, sympathy, happiness and concern for him all at the same time.

She had never felt this many things all at once before. He rubbed her silky-soft cheek. She stared as his touch excited every fiber of her being. She wanted to go slowly. He touched her hair again, but this time, he let it glide through his fingers. She noticed the spark was growing into a hot flame. Her smile deepened. Buck opened his mouth and touched her lips.

Angelique warmly allowed the kiss. She opened her mouth to meet his. Both groaned. The excitement spread through their bodies like fire, igniting emotions both have kept dormant for years. After a long kiss, Angelique pushed Buck away. They were still in the hospital cafeteria. During the kiss, they forgot where they were.

"We shouldn't do this," Angelique said.

"You're right. This is wrong."

"Buck, it's not wrong. It's just wrong right now. We're in the hospital cafeteria and your mother just died. You need to deal with that."

They sat at the table drank the tea and dunked their doughnuts. After awhile, they left.

"Angelique, a lot has happened today. I don't want to be

alone in my apartment tonight."

"Well…"

She hesitated. She didn't have much room. She
didn't want him in her bed. She wouldn't be able to control herself
if he were in her bed. Buck was too handsome and strong. The kiss
they just shared sent a fire through her that she just barely
quenched. It would be much harder at home. She vowed never to
sleep with a man until marriage. She was going to keep that pledge.
Still, Buck lost his mother and felt alone. He needed company and
comforting. She could offer both. She did have the one room.

"You can stay at the Inn. I'll tell Maggie to prepare the
room nobody ever wants."

"It's OK? You sure?"

"I have a full house. I have those from the burnt retirement
community living at my inn. But I have one room that has no view,
so we don't rent it unless it's 4th of July. So, come, stay."

"I'll pay your full rate."

"You don't have to do that. You just lost your mother. You
can come as my guest. I'll let Maggie know."

"I can pay. I have money."

"Don't worry, Buck. Many of the retirees have told me they
could be leaving soon. They are just waiting for insurance money or
money from children to arrive. So, I should be able to rent my
rooms again. I want you to stay at no charge."

"I would like that. I'll make it up to you."

"No need."

Angelique wanted to be nice, but she really could use the

money.

"Thank you. See you later."

Back at the inn, Maggie prepared the bedroom on Angelique's third floor. It was at the end of the hall near the bathroom. Although it was the only room available, Angelique knew Maggie would have put him there anyway. Maggie wasn't going to let any man sleep near her. Maggie told her many times that she wouldn't lose her innocence while Maggie was on watch. Angelique smiled. Maggie's protection never bothered her, and until now, it was never an issue. She dated but never seriously. She never brought the men back to the inn. Buck made her feel different from the others.

The bedroom hadn't been aired for many months. Neither woman saw a need to open the room. That was the one her parents always used. Few guests wanted that one because it had no view. Her parents liked the cozy feeling of the room, which was the smallest in the inn. Her mother loved the built-in fireplace in the room. She and dad would drink wine by the fire after the guests were asleep and dance to low-playing music.

Angelique preferred the one with a balcony. The small room felt cramped to her. Angelique's room was the presidential suite, but James Buchanan was the last president to stay at the inn built in the Revolutionary War era. Her parents sometimes rented the suite to bridal couples and sometimes left it open. When Angelique was young, her bedroom was the one next to her parents room, but Angelique has changed it into a room for a guest. She no longer offers the suite to couples.

Maggie and the cook slept in rooms that were once servants quarters on the first floor near the kitchen. The rest of the rooms on the second and third floors went to guests. The inn had 50 available for guests. Angelique opened a window to air the room. It was decorated in blue paisley wall paper. When she opened the window, she saw the parking lot and a chain-link fence from the store across the street behind the inn. She took an extra blanket from the closet. The room felt drafty.

Angelique heard a knock. She listened to Maggie down below.

"Ya, the guest we expectin'?"

"I'm Buck Robertson. May I come in?"

"Welcome to the 1776 Inn. Maggie's the name. I'm here to serve the guests and the friends of Miss Angelique. I want no trouble."

"Don't worry. I'm not here for trouble. My mother died tonight at the hospital. I didn't want to sleep alone in my apartment. Angelique invited me to stay here."

"Good Lord, another free guest? What is she going to do?"

"What?"

"Nothin'. I'm sorry to hear about ya mom. Poor girl lost both her parents when she was growin'. She was only in her teens. They died from a flood. This way, please."

"Angelique told me they died but didn't tell me how. What happened?"

"The storm dragged on for days, meltin' ice and snow that accumulated over the winter.

Her father was called to duty to rescue a young family swept into the river. Her father died a hero. He saved the family and their little girl, but a storm surge came and swept 'im overboard. Her mom got sick from standin' out in the rain for so long. She died a few weeks later."

"That could be why she doesn't like my job."

"Probably."

"We never use this room. Hi, Miss."
Angelique said, "Buck, welcome to the inn. We opened the window to air the room. Here is an extra blanket if you should get

cold. Philadelphia can be chilly at night in April."

"Thank you, Angelique."

"I have to leave now and buy groceries. I'll be back later. Go ahead and unpack." Maggie and Angelique walked out the room together.

* * *

Buck unpacked his things and settled for the long night ahead. He put his clothes in the antique dresser, took off his shirt and walked into the bathroom. He washed his face and arms. He felt the emptiness within himself. It's as if a part of himself had died when his mother had died. Then, Angelique had reawakened that dead part. Buck's emotions confused him. Part of him mourned his mother and another part relished the kiss with Angelique. Staying with Angelique tonight was the right move. She could calm all his fears. He couldn't live without her, but he knew that she was timid around him. During his thoughts, a hunger pain struck him. All he ate that day were the doughnuts in the hospital. He planned to ask Maggie for a sandwich later. For now, he plopped on the bed and sobbed.

# Chapter 12
*Grief at the Inn*

Eventually, Buck couldn't cry anymore. He started praying for strength. About an hour later, he decided to get that sandwich he wanted. He descended the stairs and looked for the kitchen.

"What ya need?"

"Maggie, I'm hungry. I know it's passed meal time, but could you make me a sandwich?"

"No problem."

Buck watched Maggie prepare his sandwich. Her hair extensions fell onto her shoulders. Her green eyes sparkled as she fixed the meal. He saw Maggie eyeing him. He thought it was due to his blood-shot eyes. He wouldn't tell her he had been crying. He was too macho for that. He turned his thoughts to Angelique and smiled at how her clothes accentuated her curves. Maggie caught the smile.

"Would ya like somethin' to drink?"

"Wine would be nice."

"We don't have a liquor license. You can have milk, ice tea, water, hot tea, coffee or juice."

"Milk, please."

"I'll get it."

Maggie poured the milk and handed him the sandwich. She opened a bag of chips and passed it to him.

"Thank you. Where is Angelique? I thought she said she would be back shortly."

"Now ya mention it, she should have been back. I don't know where she got to."

"I hope she's all right."

"I'm sure she went on more errands."

"Can you talk?"

"Yes, sir. I often stay with Miss Angelique. She doesn't like eating alone. She doesn't want to eat with the guests. I think she wishes she had a brother or sister."

"I know how she feels. My parents were all I had too. But, I made friends with the poor kids in my neighborhood. Now that I'm on my own, I know what an empty apartment can be like."

"Poor kids?"

"Yes. I grew up in a poor neighborhood in New York. My parents saved all they could to put me through school. They couldn't afford fancy housing. I paid for an apartment in Virginia where my school was. Then, I got a job here. They moved from New York when they retired. The retirement community where they lived burned. That's how my mother died. From complications associated with burn wounds and smoke inhalation. I don't know what my father will do now. Lindsey was his life, and he still has no place to live." Buck started to cry again but held back the tears.

Maggie patted his arm. "Don't worry. Everything will work accordin' to God's plan. Anyway, ya could put 'im up. Ya won't be alone then."

"Yes, I could. I hadn't thought about that. Right now, he's still in the hospital and I don't know if he'll live either."

He thought about Angelique living with him and thought out loud, "What if…"

Maggie changed the subject. "Ya know, I heard it was arson."

Buck stopped. "Arson?"

"Yeah. They is sayin' on the news."

"I hadn't heard that. Why?"

"Miss Angelique asked me same. They don't know or they aren't tellin'. A lot of the members of the home are here as guests. Angelique is giving them lodging."

"Can she do that?"

"It is a strain. It's dippin' into the normal business she usually gets in the spring. She feels she must do something to help."

Buck ate his sandwich and chips. He drank his milk and asked for another cup. His head hurt from crying. He asked Maggie for some pain reliever. She went into a cabinet and produced some. He thanked Maggie and headed for bed. In his room, Buck thought about his mother, father and childhood. He tried to sleep but every time he closed his eyes, he saw that body in the morgue without a smile. He shivered. Buck closed the window. He looked at the parking lot. The headlights comforted him. *I love you, Mother. Rest in peace. I'll never get any sleep if I keep thinking about her.* Pulling the covers to his chest, Buck tried to think of less emotional things.

He remembered the files and gun. Despite the warmth of the blankets, he shivered again. He should question his employees, but he did not know how to approach the subject. He did not want to scare them or admit to searching their lockers. He had to find a way to make them come to him with the information. Then, there is the suspected arson. *Why is someone trying to burn down a retirement community?* he thought. *I have to find out what's going on around here.* Buck saw a photograph of Angelique's parents and Angelique as a little girl on the night stand. Even though the picture was blurry, Angelique appeared nothing less than an angel in it. *Her parents named her right. She really is as beautiful as an angel.* Buck took the picture and caressed it. He longed to hold her in his arms and to kiss her passionately. He thought the pictured smiled back at him with the same genuine warmth that comes from Angelique's twinkling hazel eyes. Somewhere during his thoughts of Angelique, he fell asleep while holding her picture against his chest.

* * *

Angelique picked up the groceries but did not want to go back to the inn. She had somewhere to go first. She took the El to the airport. She rented a car and drove to her parents graves with flowers she bought at the store. It had been a long time since she had been there. The weeds traveled along the walls of the stones. Grass was high. Grave owners are responsible to take care of the site. She spent several hours fixing up the place after she arrived. She cried for Buck's mother. She cried for Buck's father. She cried for her parents. She cried for Buck. She cried because Mr. Kennedy felt her in places he shouldn't have.

"I'm sorry, Mom. I'm sorry, Dad. I wish I told you I loved you. I'm not managing the inn as well as you did."

She sat there until the care taker arrived.

"Miss, you're not allowed here after dark. You must go."

She left but still did not go back to the inn. She drove around the city for awhile. She glanced at the clock on the dashboard. It said 10:45 p.m. Angelique started crying. She wiped her tears away and drove. She concentrated on the road.

"Don't worry, Mr. Robertson. Everything will be OK," she said to herself.

She was tired but thought about her inn. She liked her bed and breakfast because she didn't have to deal with death so much. She liked the tourists' smiles. She liked the hope she saw, the love she saw. She kept thinking of Stanley losing his beloved wife. She thought about Buck losing his mother. Angelique empathized with Buck. Losing parents is the most difficult event to face in life. A horrifying thought occurred to her. *What if Buck died? What would I do? He could never die. He's too young and healthy. But he works on the river. Dad was not that old when he died on the river.* Buck was almost perfect. His tanned muscles broadly attaching to his perfect neck and his gorgeous brown eyes. *If only, he would quit the cruise line business*, she thought. Angelique remembered his smile like that of an innocent little boy. She shivered at the thought of an innocent little boy. That boy she saw when she was so young popped into her head. She decided it was time to go back to the inn. She knew Buck would be asleep before she got there.
It was well past midnight when Angelique arrived at her bed and breakfast. She was emotionally drained. She could not take much more pain and suffering, first the retirement community and now death. She checked on Buck and lumbered to bed.

# Chapter 13
## *The Plans*

While Buck slept at the inn, Mr. Kennedy opened the door to the office at 11 p.m. He hoped Buck had left for the evening. He didn't want another encounter with his manager. He wished he never hired him. Buck concerned himself too much with his business. Yet, Mr. Kennedy needed someone to take care of the daily routine while he conducted his work. He didn't want to sit all day in a cramped office routing through and filing paper work. That's one of the pleasures of being an owner. But, Kennedy regretted his decision. He wanted someone intelligent with a degree as manager, but Kennedy now thinks he should have picked someone dumb who would not question his decisions. Someone who could not discover the missing money.

Buck will eventually figure out what is happening at the pier. Mr. Kennedy will not allow Buck to discover his handiwork. He'll have to frame someone and get rid of the nasty manager once and for all. Mr. Kennedy remembered Angelique witnessed his transaction. *Maybe, she'll have to die as well! She's way too nosy.* Mr. Kennedy had more pressing matters to handle at the moment. He needed to get the material from the office. He plans to hock it as soon as it is collected. Then, Buck won't find it.

"Curses. I would have had it earlier if it wasn't for that Miss Chalfonte and her lover of a manager."

Mr. Kennedy sat in a the chair wrinkling his black suit. He nervously tapped the desk with his office keys. Perspiring, Mr. Kennedy took off his jacket and loosened his tie. He unlocked the filing cabinet and took out an envelope. The envelope had a key. Mr. Kennedy opened a safe behind the ticket counter that was hidden by brochure racks. The safe held several bags of a white substance.

Tapping his keys again, he tried to think. His mind had too many problems for him to think clearly. He sat. Minutes ticked into hours. All of a sudden, Mr. Kennedy found a way to disguise what he was doing. In the ships' computer logs, Mr. Kennedy recorded private party trips anywhere a cruise had been canceled. Buck would believe it was. He had already used that excuse once. Mr. Kennedy's worries eased a little for now. He still needed to find someone to frame for the murder of his manager and his lovely woman. He closed the log book with a thud and shoved it back on the desk under Buck's pile of papers. He locked the safe again and headed out the door. Mr. Kennedy steered toward the alley several blocks from the office. When he arrived, he called someone. While waiting for his party, Mr. Kennedy paced the bricks in the street. He unbuttoned his shirt. Someone pointed a gun at him. Mr. Kennedy put his hands in his pockets touching the gun he always carried. He caressed his gun but left it where it was. The two men stood in dark shadows.

"Give me the stuff," the person demanded.

"Where's my money?" Kennedy asked.

"Don't have it yet."
"No money. No goods."

"Unfair."

"You have until noon. No later."

"OK noon. Where?"

"The old warehouse on Delaware Avenue."

The man left. Mr. Kennedy suddenly got nervous. Now he had to stash the goods again. His nosy manager could find it before he could retrieve it tomorrow. Every moment he held the stuff put him in more danger of someone finding out his scheme. Mr. Kennedy walked for hours along the river, trying to decide where to stash the stuff until noon tomorrow. He saw his ship and knew there was a loose panel behind the door that houses life jackets. He decided to put the stuff there. He kept walking. He was agitated. He knew he couldn't sleep. *Why bother going home?* He had to develop a plan to get himself out of this mess. The first part was accomplished with the log books. He could not figure out how to get the goods once he stashed it. The ship would be sailing at noon. Somehow, he would have to get his manager to leave the office early in the morning and to keep the ship at dock. He walked to the dock and cut the fuel line of the ship where he hid his materials. *I'll tell Mr. Robertson to go to the repair yard and bring a maintenance crew back to the dock to fix the fuel line. Then I can get my stuff.*

Mr. Kennedy pondered how to kill the snoopy manager and the owner of the inn. He also had to get rid of evidence before criminal investigators could find his misdeeds. When he reached the pool hall, Mr. Kennedy stared at the building. *I can find a patsy in there for sure!* Mr. Kennedy smirked. He had more confidence now. He continued walking, but this time, he held his head straight.

# Chapter 14
*The Alibi*

Tired from walking, Mr. Kennedy entered the local tavern. He sat on a bar stool and asked for whiskey. The bar tender filled a shot glass.

"Give me the whole bottle," he barked.

The bar tender nodded and went to serve other customers. Mr. Kennedy sat on his stool drinking whiskey shots. He repeated "Got to kill 'em" constantly. As he sat two bar thugs started shoving each other.

"I said you cheat!"

"I don't cheat, you scum. You are just sore you can't play cards worth a damn!"

"What did you say?"

"You heard me. Or are ya deaf as well as stupid?"

"That does it."

Pow! The two men broke chairs and bottles. Mr. Kennedy laughed. He enjoyed this break in reality. The scuffle continued until the tavern bouncer threw the two men to the curb. The bar tender began cleaning the place. Mr. Kennedy poured another shot. He stared at the bottle. His thoughts drifted to his early life.

His father often got into bar fights over cheating. His father claimed that he never cheated, but Franklin knew better. The little boy would come to the gambling room and watch his father. Once, the young Mr. Kennedy blabbed his father's scheme accidentally. He got so excited when he saw that his father had four kings.

Young Franklin jumped up and down screaming, "You'll never catch my daddy!" The other men folded and looked at the cards. They realized they were being scammed. The men chased Mr. Kennedy's father who grabbed his son and ran away from the bar. At home, his father slammed the door and stripped his belt. He pulled down Franklin's pants and belted him with the wide strap until young Franklin's body had black and blue marks all over it. Every time the child cried, he received more strokes.

"Don't you ever do that again! You cost me the game! I needed that money and you spoiled it! You're such a sissy boy! Grow up!"

Fearing more blows, Franklin backed into a corner and stared at his father. "I won't. I promise."

"Go to your room."

That experience hardened Mr. Kennedy. He could no longer see the good in people. He never again gave away his father's secret. He instead decided to learn as much about his father's trade as possible. He started simply by scamming children to give him their chore money. As he grew, his schemes became more complex and lucrative. He achieved his wealth by traveling with a medicine man, a person who took land money from senior citizens by selling miracle cures. The cures had nothing but sugar, water and whiskey. All brands had the same ingredients. Eventually, the owner of the medicine man show died and gave it all to Mr. Kennedy. He traveled until a federal investigator saw through his scheme.

Mr. Kennedy decided he needed a legitimate business to hide the underhanded scams he pulled. Mr. Kennedy read in the paper that he could buy a cruise ship line from an auction for a fraction of its worth. He never really mastered the poker face that his father did so well. As a result, he lost as many scams as he won. Lately, he kept losing. His father taught him never to leave the table until he wins, and he plans to do just that. *The fools. Getting rid of them will be easy. My tide will turn then.* All these memories caused his head to spin. He needed a woman to take away the headache. Mr. Kennedy's father also taught Franklin how to get a woman and how to use one. The lad's mother died in child birth. So, his father would often bring prostitutes home to bed.

After getting his thrill, his father would grab them and force them to make him a meal and clean house. Sometimes, he sent them to please the teen-age Franklin. If the woman refused, his father would give them a taste of the belt he gave Franklin. Eventually, word would spread to the other women that they better not refuse the man.

Franklin Kennedy takes what he wants from women too. Instead of a belt, he uses his hands and a knife when it comes to that. Mr. Kennedy saw the one he wanted. Trixie. Her breasts heaved with each breath in that tight dress. Her fishnet stockings flowed up her legs like a raging river. Mr. Kennedy's thighs ached as he followed her stockings to the top. When she bent over the tables, her round bottom wiggled. Mr. Kennedy joined the rest of the bar in making animal sounds toward her.

Throwing money on the bar, Mr. Kennedy walked over to Trixie. He rubbed her bottom to get her attention. Trixie turned and looked at Mr. Kennedy.

"Yeah?"

"I want you."

"Yeah? What you got?"

"Money. Own Delaware River Touring Co."

"Oooo Baby. Let's go."

Trixie and Mr. Kennedy entered the back room where she gave him all his fantasies. Anything he wanted, she provided. Trixie and Mr. Kennedy continued the sex all night long. Mr. Kennedy hurt Trixie by playing rough just as his father had taught him. Trixie did not scream. She was a professional. Trixie understood that pain was part of her job. The money paid for all the pain. If she could continue pleasing Mr. Kennedy, he might make Trixie his personal girl, which would net much more. About the same time that Trixie considered this concept, Mr. Kennedy thought he could use Trixie as a way to kill the two thorns in his operation. He could control her. Mr. Kennedy could force her to go along with his plans. If she refused, she'll have a taste of the man he really is.

"Baby, you're great. I want you to stay with me until I say

you can go."

"Oooo, baby!"

Mr. Kennedy had all his plans in the works. Next step action. Right now, his head still ached.

"Give me more!" he barked. He rubbed her legs and fondled her breasts. Trixie kissed him with a sloppy kiss. His breath smelled of whiskey, but she didn't care. Thrust after thrust, Trixie worked him. At dawn, Mr. Kennedy seemed satisfied. Mr. Kennedy went to the office to inform Buck about the fuel line but did not find him. He told Roxy to cancel the 10 o'clock ship because it needed a new fuel line. She did not question the order and canceled the tour. Later, Kennedy got what he wanted.

# Chapter 15
## *Almost Heaven*

About five o'clock in the morning, Buck woke. He tossed and turned all night. He vaguely remembered someone standing in the door way, checking on him. He knew it had to be Angel, but he was too worn out to notice. Buck stared at the ceiling listening to the sounds of dawn. A clock downstairs chimed the quarter hour. The wind whistled against the window. The wind was blowing stronger, a sign that another storm was coming. He thought about Angel. Her long legs reminded him of silk. Her eyes danced every time he held her. Her smiled warmed him like hot cocoa even on the coldest and wettest days. He knew. *I love you, Angelique.* He also knew that he was in no position to take her as his wife. She didn't like his job. He didn't have enough. He still had his mission. He could not tell her his secret. And, he could die doing his job.

* * *

Despite exhaustion, Angelique stayed awake all night thinking about Buck who slept down the hall. He was so beautiful when she checked on him. His hair drizzled over the pillow like sea weed on the beach. His body took over the entire bed but there was a gentleness about it. She could see that whatever roughness he displayed during the day left him when he slept. She longed for him. She had read books about how the first time was so magical if you loved someone. *Was Maggie right? Do I love him? I hope not.*

However, Angelique was not about to relinquish her virginity before she was married. Several men have tried to get inside her when she was not ready. She assumed Buck would be like all the others. Angelique thought about the days she has known him. He made the lousy days seem not so lousy because they were together. Somehow, Angelique fell asleep around 5 a.m. only to be awaken by a loud piercing noise. *The smoke alarms!* There was crackling and she coughed from inhaling smoke. *Oh no fire!* She raced downstairs through a smoke-filled hallway. She pounded on the doors and told everyone to exit as quickly as possible. Buck had grabbed the fire extinguisher and sprayed it on the flames. Angelique called the fire department. Maggie and the cook heard the alarms and ran out the back door. They waited with the guests.

Maggie said a prayer for Angelique who had not exited the building. This was the second fire for most of them. The fire department arrived.

"The fire's out," Buck said.

"We'll check and assess damage," the lieutenant said. "The fire is indeed out, but most of the damage is on the third floor. It looks like it started in the hallway near the presidential suite bedroom. Fires don't normally start in bedrooms. This is likely arson. Are you having any financial trouble?"

"What? You think I started this fire? For the insurance money?

Are you crazy?" Angelique said.

"We have to investigate every possibility."

"Well, when you investigate, you'll see I sold my insurance policy to pay the bills last week. If the place goes up in smoke, so does my business."

"You have no insurance?" Buck asked.

Angelique cried. "No, I don't. I was going to get a policy again next month after I have gotten some income. Now, I have all this damage to fix."

"Angelique…"

"Don't say anything. I can manage. It's not your problem."

"I still think it was arson."

"Maybe, it was the same person who burned the retirement community," Buck said.

"Could be. In any case, we'll investigate. The guests can come back."

"The fire's out. It's safe to come back inside the building now," Buck said.

"Thank the Lord," Maggie sighed.

Maggie, the cook and the guests headed back to their rooms, leaving Buck and Angelique alone in the drawing room. Maggie and the cook began making breakfast for the guests.

"Thanks. You saved my inn. One fire is all I can take. I'm sorry this incident woke you," Angelique said.

"I couldn't sleep anyway. I was about to get up and exercise before showering."

"Sorry to hear you couldn't sleep. I hope it wasn't the bed."

Angelique tried to act businesslike.

Buck shrugged. "I had things on my mind."

"Me too."

"You mean you couldn't sleep either? Well, you're probably worrying about many things."

"I was but I fell asleep right before the alarm sounded."

"I couldn't stop thinking about how much I loved you," Buck said with an air of hope.

"Buck, I think…"

"You're everything I want in a wife."

"I think I love you too, but everything is happening so fast between us."

"Don't push me away. I need you Angel."

"Did you say, 'Angel?'"

"Yes. Angelique is too long. And you're as pretty as an angel."

"No one ever called me that but my Mom."

"Well now I have."

Buck grabbed her. He kissed her long and hard. She couldn't breathe, but she did not care. All she wanted was more. He pulled her at arms length.

"You look sexy in your night gown."

"You're not bad yourself in your T-shirt and briefs. Buck, kiss me more."

Smiling, Buck pulled her close again. He let his tongue dance with hers. Their breathing became short and heavy. Angelique arched her back in his touch. She got hot. She didn't know if it was the heat in the building or her. Buck moved his tongue down her neck. This sent a shock wave through her. Her toes tingled. Buck guided Angelique to the floor. She wore a halo of chemicals from the extinguisher but didn't notice it. Buck's kisses made her think of nothing else. His tongue glided over her soft shoulders. Meanwhile, he grasped her long, silky legs. He moved his hand up one and down the other. He couldn't contain himself. Her legs called out to him. He rubbed her underwear, forcing Angelique to scream. She pushed him hard against the floor. Buck looked startled and puzzled.

"What's wrong? I thought you enjoyed what I was doing?"

Angelique's red eyes were once again wet. "I do. I just can't do what you want me to do."

"Am I too rough?" Buck asked remembering the scared look she had the day Kennedy was in his office.

"No, you're gentle as a lamb. It's just that everything that has happened. The two fires, the death, the day in your office, the day in the hospital, the finances. It's all too much too fast. I can't go on at this pace."

"Angelique, we'll go slow. When you're ready, you'll know. We'll feel the passion that is between us now. I care about you too much to force you to do something you are not ready for."

"Buck, thank you for understanding. I just want to wait for marriage."

At that, Buck cringed. "I don't think I can marry you."

Angelique thought he was a typical male who just wanted to get the milk for free without the commitment. "I thought you said 'I'm everything you want in a wife. That you love me.' Or is that a line you throw out to every woman, you want to bed?"

"No, it isn't. It's complicated. I…"

She would not let him finish. She stormed up the stairs and slammed her door.

# Chapter 16
## *The Funeral*

Buck stayed at the inn for several more days but avoided Angelique. He sensed she did not want to deal with him. But he could not bear to be alone in his apartment, so he arranged the funeral from the inn. He was afraid about being away from the office for so long. On the one hand, he had a job to do. On the other hand, he could be fired. However, he had to deal with his mother's death. *I'll deal with Kennedy when I get back.*

He notified his mother's friends, her sister and his father's brother and wife. He called friends who lived in New York, about 20 in all, and asked Angelique if they could stay at her inn. Angelique had three rooms available but said she would squeeze them somehow. Buck knew this would put even more financial strain on Angelique. He was worried about her but decided against talking to her about it because Angelique was still angry with him. Buck visited the funeral parlor to make arrangements for the viewing and funeral. He picked a nice casket made of maple. His mother always liked the dark brown woods. He did not know what dress she could wear. He was not allowed in her apartment as a criminal investigation was under way. Some of her things burned in the fire.

"She can have my dress. I have extra," Maggie said.

"Thanks Maggie, but I don't know if that will feel right. Mom's friends might not recognize it as her," Buck said between sobs.

He was not making sense to Maggie, but she knew how much it means to a person to have the perfect dress for a funeral.

"There, there, Mr. Buck. We'll find her the perfect dress. Let me make you tea."

Buck sat on the couch in the drawing room. Some of the guests came into the room and opened their books. Others pitied him, remembering their friends who also died in the fire.

"Your mother was a good woman, always cared about the rest of us," said Mrs. O'Reilly, a plump woman with sandy-gray hair. She looked like Mrs. Mateo. "We're all coming tomorrow."

"Thanks."

"I heard you talking to the housekeeper that you need a dress. My sister has one to lend your mother. I'm sure Lindsey would love it."

"And, your sister is…"

"Lindsey's best friend, Mrs. Mateo."

"Of course!" Buck said smiling.

"All my things burned of course, but hers'll do."

"I'd appreciate that. Now, if I could figure out what to do about my father. The hospital says he's not strong enough to leave even for a few hours. But I know he'll want to be there or he'll feel guilty."

"We'll figure somethin'."

Buck sat in silence for awhile. The guests returned to their books. Maggie brought the tea. He sipped in silence. He thought about his mother. She always brought him cookies and something to drink when he was upset. In the winter, she brought hot chocolate. In the summer, she brought lemonade. He missed her terribly. *How am I supposed to say good-bye to her tomorrow?*

\* \* \*

Angelique offered to keep the tours going so Buck did not have that worry. It was a way to be far from Buck. She did not know what to do about the paperwork. She sent the information to a friend of her mother's who was an accountant. She did what she could to keep everything current. The day before the funeral, Angelique decided to clean the ships. They were out on the river late, and she sent the crew home without cleaning them.

"Roxy, can you help me?"

"Sure, Miss."

"I'll sweep below if you mop the upper deck. We'll meet in the middle for the final cleaning. Then, we'll polish the hand rails."

"'Kay."

Roxy took the mop up the stairs of the boat. Angelique descended the stairs to the cabin floor. She cleaned out the trash in the bins. She collected the newspapers for recycling. She threw out leftover drinks and bits of food left on paper plates. She moved chairs and grabbed a broom. She saw a strange thing under the last table closest to the kitchen. The table was marked reserved for crew members. When she got closer, she realized the strange thing was a compartment that held a padlock on it.

"That's odd. Tourist boats don't usually have compartments in the hull. Those are for fishing boats. And, locked compartments are usually near the captain's room not the kitchen," she said out loud to herself. Something about it nagged at her. Something her father used to talk about, but she couldn't remember. "Oh, well," she sighed.

She was about to climb the stairs when she heard a sound like a knocking. She figured it was nerves and climbed the stairs.

"Roxy, did you hear anything strange a few minutes ago?"

"Like what?"

"I thought I heard knocking."

"Oh that. This boat always makes those sounds when it's docked. I think it's the movement of the river."

"I see. I guess you would know."

"When's Mr. Robertson coming back?"

"Probably in two days. Tomorrow's the funeral."

"Got it. Poor guy, losing his mother. Have they caught the guy that set the fire?"

"I haven't heard anything. Probably not or it would be all over the news."

"Yeah. Right," she said as she chewed gum loudly. Hours passed. Angelique returned before the last boat sailed. She said Roxy could do it. The workers knew what they had to do. Most could not speak English, but Roxy could speak Spanish. She found Buck in the drawing room.

"Buck?"

"Mmmm," was his answer.

"Are you all right?"

"Just dandy. My mom's funeral is tomorrow. My dad is in the hospital. I don't know if I have a job when I get back. And you ask a stupid question?"

Buck snapped at her, which stung. Angelique asked, "What can I do for you?"

Her eyes filled with tears, but she was concerned for him. He felt guilty about snapping at her. He was glad she was there to help him and was helping at the pier.

"I need a way to get my father to the funeral."

"Maybe we need to bring the funeral to him instead of the other way around."

"What do you mean?"

"We move the funeral to the chapel in the hospital. We'll tell everyone where to go."

"That might work. Angel, I'm..."

"Save it. I lost my parents too. And, you should not call me Angel."

That night, Angelique was busy checking people into her inn. She doubled several guests into the three rooms. She asked Buck's aunt and uncle to sleep in his room. His other aunt slept with her. She asked some of the guests from the fire to double up and put cots in the drawing room for the remaining people staying for the funeral. They would only be there for two nights. The next day everyone at the bed and breakfast got ready for the funeral. The only ones not going were the true tourists, the five people who stayed at the bed and breakfast for the pleasure of seeing the city. Everyone else were either guests of Buck or residents of the retirement community. Angelique told the funeral home and the minister to conduct the funeral at the chapel in the hospital. The funeral home kept a person at the church to tell people to go the hospital.

* * *

Buck left early to help his father be at the chapel for his mother. The funeral home driver took Buck to the hospital. He tried to be strong for Stanley.

"Dad, are you ready?"

"Thank you Buck for doing this."

"It was Angelique's idea."

"That lady who has brought us flowers?"

"Yes."

"I like her."

"She doesn't like me. And, this is not the time."

"She reminds me of your mother when she was young."

"Let's get you in a wheel chair."

Buck wheeled his father down the hall into the chapel. The minister talked about Lindsey's life. He praised her faith, her kindness and her willingness to do everything she could for family. Angelique sat there listening but the words brought back memories of the funeral for her mother. Her father's funeral was a military one and much more formal. She liked the intimate one better. Angelique remembered she wore a black skirt and a white top. She did not have anything black when her mother died. She had worn the same outfit for her father's funeral. Her mother's friends attended but filled only the first three pews. Her grandmother attended even though she had Alzheimer's disease and was supposed to be in the nursing home.

Her grandmother had moments when she could understand what happened and moments when she could not. Angelique appreciated her being there. The priest talked about Jacqueline's life. He said she served others and brightened everyone's day. She treated her guests fairly and always did what she could to help those in need. Angelique started to cry, which brought her back to Lindsey's funeral. She scanned the chapel. She could see Buck was having trouble standing still. He looked like he wanted Angelique to hold his hand and comfort him the way she comforted his father, but she sat four rows behind him. She did not want to be near him.

Buck cried as he remembered Lindsey's life and smile. Angelique saw the tears and shook her head. She missed her mother and felt bad for Buck. She knew exactly how Buck felt at that moment. She would not tell him. He would not care. He just wanted her for her body. After the service, everyone except Stanley went back to the inn for refreshments. Buck mingled and reminisced about Lindsey. Problems at work were far from Buck's mind, but they were going to come back when he opened the office.

# Chapter 17
## *The Arrangements*

Mr. Kennedy met his buyer at the warehouse on Delaware Avenue.

"Got my money?"

The man pushed a briefcase toward Mr. Kennedy. He scooped up the case, opened it, counted the money and threw several packages at him.

"I have another shipment coming tonight."

"So soon? I won't get money that fast."

"You have a week to get the money per our agreement. How you get it is your problem not mine. Too many people are sniffing around my operations. I can't hold onto it too long," Kennedy shouted.

"How am I to get that much that fast?"

"Steal it for all I care! Be here in one week!"

He left. He grabbed the briefcase and smiled. He owed this money to someone, but he decided to use it for something else. He visited the pool hall. He watched the clientele until he found the right patsy. The man was large, about 300 pounds, muscular and desperately in need of money. Kennedy plunked $50,000 on the table in front of him.

"This could be yours if you do a little job for me," he sneered.

"What sort of job?" the man said with a deep voice.

Kennedy showed the man two pictures via a folder.

"These have to go. Make it an accident. Make sure it happens at night. I have an alibi lined up for nights."

"When?"

"As soon as possible."

Kennedy left $1,000 on the table and the folders. He took back the rest as the man was about to grab it. "You get more when you finished."

"Yes sir."

Kennedy had stolen the man's car keys. He had made a second set of folders. He wore ski gloves even though the temperature was around 70 degrees. He opened the trunk and slipped the folders inside the car. He left to find Trixie. He had a couple of hours before he met his men for his next shipment, which he'll hide in the same place. *It will be safe there for a week*, he thought. He also had to remove his cargo from the hull and deal with it.

"Come here," he bellowed at Trixie.

"Yeah?"

"Back room, now."

"Sure honey."

"You have to a do a job for me. You can't say no or you get no more of my money. Got it?"

A little frightened but more curiously, Trixie said, "Anything you say, Baby."

"You are going to be with me every night until I tell you otherwise. You are to pretend to be my girlfriend. I want pleasure." *But mostly, I want an alibi*, he thought. "You'll get paid handsomely. You will also seduce my manager and make Miss Angelique Chalfonte jealous." *That way, he'll be more likely to take the fall.*

"And, what do I get for that?"

"You get me, you Bitch!" Then he slapped her so hard she fell into the table. "Didn't I just say, you'd be paid for it?"

"Yeah," she said catching her balance. Her face stung. "You seduce my manager tomorrow."

"Yeah, sure."

Kennedy stripped off his clothes and ripped hers. He laid on the couch naked. Trixie came over and sat on top. She started pleasuring him all over his body. She did whatever he asked as long as he wanted. He was a long-term paying job so she did not care how humiliating or rough Kennedy was. She kept going even though she was exhausted from all the rough thrusts inside her. Trixie's legs ached from being straddled open so long. Her insides burned, but she continued pleasing him.

"That's enough," Kennedy said at midnight. "I have to be somewhere. As far as you're concerned I didn't leave until dawn."

Trixie nodded. Kennedy threw several hundred dollar bills at her. "There's more where that came from."

She nodded again. She began to put her ripped clothes back on her body. Kennedy cupped her naked bottom one last time and left. He met his men in secret at a deserted warehouse near the stadiums. He did not want anyone to find them.

"Did everything go OK tonight?"

"Si, Señor Kennedy."

"Where is the stash?"

"We put it in the safe as always."

"Good. I'll move it later."

"We have a new shipment due on Saturday's cruise. Be ready."

"Señor, Saturday es busy day. Won't they get spicious?" asked Enrique Bañal.

"No they won't. It's my job to take care of that. Your job is to get it on the ship."

"Si, Señor Kennedy."

"What do we do about the cargo in the hull?"

"I'm working on that. Ritchie, do you have the papers?"

"Yes." He handed him papers for the people in the hull. "Make sure you cover up the excursion like last time."

"No problem."

Kennedy gave Enrique money for the shipment. "As usual, you take your cut after the shipment arrives. Oh and give yourself a little of the prize too," he said grinning mischievously. Two teeth were missing.

"Si, Señor."

"We have a new problem. I have hired someone to deal with that problem. He will need help. Do whatever he asks. Got it?"

"Yes," said Ritchie.

"Si," said Enrique.

"Good."

Kennedy left them and headed for his touring ship. He unlocked the hull and let out several frightened Cubans who had not eaten in a long time. He gave them water and small slices of bread. He then handed them papers and motioned to them to follow. Kennedy led them through the streets of Philadelphia to a small house in the Hispanic neighborhood. The house had not been painted in 10 years and had one bedroom. It had a wooden fence around it that was falling apart.

Weeds overtook the grass, which was four inches higher than it should have been. Windows were dirty with ripped curtains. Kennedy knocked. The Spanish woman who answered looked like Enrique and wore torn dress with faded flowers on it and carried two babies. Another child hid behind her legs. They were all up despite the lateness.

"Here, Rosetta. These are the newest arrivals," Kennedy told her. He pushed them at her.

"I still got 20 here from last month's trip. I can't find them no work. And Belinda still hasn't had the baby so she can stay."

"Do I care about your problems? I get them here. That's all I do. That's the deal. What you do with them is your business."

"I still haven't been paid."

Kennedy yanked her straggly and braided black hair. "You'll get your money when I have it to give to you. Not one day sooner! I have too many losses at work to give you money!"

He stormed away from her laughing. He knew he had the money he could give her.

# Chapter 18
## *Odd Accounting*

Buck returned to work hoping to avoid Mr. Kennedy. He wanted to get caught up on paperwork and sniff around the office. He started with the ships' databases.

"Roxy, please come here."

"Sir?"

"The computer lists private cruise several times. Do you know anything?"

"Mr. Kennedy told me he rented the boat for private parties. That's all I know."

"Thank you. This doesn't match the proceeds. The accounting databases don't show any rental fees received."

"That's weird." She frowned for a moment. "Hey, I thought you said money is missing."

"True."

"Well that money must be the fees for the private parties."

"Could be."

"Can I go now?"

"Sure, Roxy."

Buck knew the missing money was not from Mr. Kennedy forgetting to record rental fees from private parties. He knew that Kennedy was using the ships illegally, but he did not know why. He knew Kennedy probably took that money. *But why?* Buck is getting closer to the truth. To avoid questions from Kennedy, Buck fixed the accounting databases to record $3,000 wherever a private voyage had taken place without payment being recorded. Buck began tearing apart the office looking for any clue to what Kennedy was doing. He searched the desk. He searched the walls. He searched the floor. All he found was a  small piece of paper with accident written on it. That made no sense to Buck. He did not like it at all. A shiver went down his spine.

Buck left his office. He casually walked through the reception area, glancing at items where he could without looking suspicious. He noticed the brochure rack was not against the wall as usual. Walking to the rack and pulling out one flyer on horse-and-buggy rides, he hid his face. He glanced over the brochure to see a safe behind the counter. He had no idea what the combination was. He knew Kennedy must have something in there he does not want anyone to find. On the floor by the rack, Buck found a piece of paper with numbers on it and "From the desk of Trixie." He pocketed the paper and went back to his office.

Knock. Knock.

Buck jumped. "Enter."

"Buck, here are today's bookings. None of them are full," Roxy said.

"Two cruises are only one-quarter capacity. That won't give us enough profits. Mr. Kennedy'll be storming mad."

"People are concerned. They heard of funny business here."

"Funny business?"

"You know." She blew a long bubble. "Trips being canceled at the last minute. No refunds. Ships out half the night. Some going out in severe storms."

"I see. We need to fill up these seats. Call the 8 o'clock and see if they'll take the 10 in the morning or 4 o'clock trips. Then cancel the 8 o'clock."

"Yes sir. By the way, yesterday, Miss Chalfonte thought she heard a strange noise in the ships. I told her not to worry."

"What sort of noise?"

"A knocking. I told her I hear the ship making that sound all the time."

"How often?"

"Don' know. Never paid attention. Maybe, once a month."
"OK, you may go."

Buck wondered about the noise. He did not believe it was the boat when it occurred only once a month. It could be the boat hitting the dock, but something told him it was not. He had to figure out how to confront the two employees. He started doodling on a piece of paper. He drew a gun and files and began tapping his pen. *What were they doing? How can I find out?* Buck dialed the phone.

"Yeah. I need to search it. I know it has something to do with the mission." He paused.

"How am I to get permission?" He paused again.

"Well if that's the way it has to be." He hung up the phone and decided he needed a new plan. Buck opened his filing cabinet. Just as he suspected more files had disappeared. He opened a drawer and opened a file. He wrote his notes. He put the piece of paper from Trixie, the piece of paper with accident on it and the information about the mysterious noise in a folder. He hid the file under workmen's compensation forms in his drawer. He went to process the ships for sailing.

# Chapter 19
## *Sabotage*

Angelique sat in her office working at the computer. Maggie entered.

"Room 3 is complaining of a running toilet. I tried to stop it, but somethin's wrong."

"That is the third complaint this morning. Call a plumber. We'll have him check all the rooms. The guests might be inconvenienced, but it would save us in the long run."

"Yes, Miss Angelique."

"We've never had this many problems before now. I wonder what is going on."

"I think the moon is outa whack. It seems to happen every full moon."

"Minor stuff and weird stuff yes, but always stuff we can fix. The things happening are troubles we can't fix. If we keep having problems like this, we'll have to close."

"Ah hope not, Miss."

"Don't worry, Maggie. You'll always have a home here."
"Ah not worried 'bout that. Ah is worried 'bout ya. Ya know nothin' else. This is causing ya stress."

"I'll be fine. I opened my home to strangers. Isn't that what God asks us to do? I'm sure things will get better."

"Ah hope ya right, Miss Angelique."

"Maggie, please take care of the plumbing. I need to be alone."

"Yes, Miss."

Angelique was not fine. She was stressed. She had trouble sleeping. The funeral brought back too many unpleasant memories. Her business that her parents carefully built was failing. She has lost many customers because of all that has happened. She also was not getting the recommendations from Kennedy due to her letter. He may be a creep, but he knows a lot of executives. Other companies have failed to produce the necessary recommendations. She had to take action to save her inn.

Despite all that stress, she had a nagging feeling Buck was in danger. She missed him a lot. Having him at the inn brightened her day even though she was mad at him. She also thought someone had stalked her.

"That was ridiculous. Who would be watching me?" she asked herself even though she knew the answer.

As she worked, her danger radar was on high alert. Angelique continued inputting the week's receipts into the computer, ordered food for the kitchen, searched for new recipes or decorating ideas, and created a flyer for the kiosk at the Philadelphia Convention and Visitor's Bureau. That should help. At least, she could do that without paying any more money she did not have. At lunchtime, Angelique took the flyer to the kiosk and afterward decided to see if Buck wanted to eat with her at a restaurant near the pier. She needed to relax. Buck was not in his office. She did not look for him. She instead walked along Penn's Landing. She was nervous. She heard noises but assumed they were nothing. She thought she was imagining things. She stepped into The Water Front, a small restaurant that allows customers to watch the river and all its activity.

"Table for one?" asked the hostess.

"Yes. One away from the window, please."

"Sure thing. This way." The skinny strawberry-blonde led her to a table in the back against a wall. She handed Angelique a menu. She scanned the menu. She saw the menu had advertisements for local lodging on it.

"What is this?"

"We accept advertising for local bed and breakfasts in a trade agreement. The bed and breakfast has to put advertising for our restaurant somewhere prominent in its place," the waitress said.

"I noticed that none of the large hotels are listed."

"No. We only do local places. National chains don't need the extra advertisements."

"I own the 1776 Inn."

"My manager loves that place. She has stayed there a few times and enjoys the receptions you have. You should definitely advertise."

"Can I talk to the manager?"

"No she is not here today. I'll give her your business card."

"That would be great."

Angelique felt a little better. About 10 minutes later, a man in a trench coat entered. He kept his face hidden. He took a table in the front. He looked at the water and occasionally glanced at Angelique. He wanted to learn her habits. The information would prove useful to him and his boss. He smiled at himself. The damage he caused at the inn will not be fixed easily. The inn will be out of commission for several days at least. Many of the guests will have no where to go since the retirement community burned. Angelique will not be able to trust Mr. Robertson when she finds out he did this. Mr. Robertson would not be able to trust her when he finds out she threw out those people without a home. The first part of his boss' plan was completed.

Angelique ordered a chef's salad with an order of bread sticks. She felt like she was being watched. Her hairs stood on end. After lunch, she walked back to the inn. She had not relaxed as she had hoped. She needed Buck, but he had work to do. She needed to save her inn and could not waste time going to him. At least, she could advertise with the restaurant. When she returned to the inn, her spirits sank again as she received bad news.

"Can't fix it," the plumber said. "Several of the pipes are clogged or broken. Many will burst at any minute."

"What could have caused all this?" Angelique said.

"It was deliberately done. Oh, I found these files in several pipes."

He handed them to Angelique. Property of the Delaware River Touring Co. was printed on them. Inside were soggy papers of trips taken and employees on those routes, but she could not read anything beyond that. She did notice Buck's signature on one paper.

"I'll have to rip out the whole system and start from scratch It'll take a week," said the bearded plumber who was tall and spoke with a gruff voice. His brown hair had specks of gray in them and his fingers were larger than normal for a man.

"A week? What am I supposed to do without plumbing for a week? What about my guests? They need a place to stay."

"Don't know miss. But the damage is too extensive to do in a day. I'll hire a crew and be here tomorrow first thing. Bye."

Angelique sank in a chair. She had to make everyone go and refund the paying guests. Anger grew inside her. *How could Buck have done this to me after what I did for him? I knew there was something mysterious about him. He wanted to stay here to sabotage me. He must have done it for that evil Kennedy. There is no other explanation.* With tears in her eyes, she began to knock on doors to tell the guests the bad news. Maggie helped.

# Chapter 20
## *The Seduction*

Buck almost left the office for the night. He was tired and in pain. The rain dripped past his face. All he wanted to do was go home to his apartment to take a nice hot bath. But someone had knocked on his door. Buck felt hairs rise on his skin. It was 11:30 p.m. Roxy had gone home hours ago. Buck assumed Mr. Kennedy wanted something.

"Come in," he said reluctantly.

The door opened to reveal a short woman with dirty-blonde curly hair. It was cut like a bob and draped her face. Her slender torso and long, boney legs would make any man crave her. She wore a purple halter top and brown shorts. Her nipples were clearly visible under the top as she did not wear a bra. Although most men would have jumped her right then, Buck was not like most men.

"We are not running any tours just now. Come back

tomorrow."

"I don't want to schedule a tour. Mr. Kennedy said you were lonely. I'm here to make you happy."

Trixie walked closer to Buck.

"Miss, I'm not interested."

"Trixie. That's my name. Mr. Kennedy said you work too hard." She stood two inches from Buck's face. Trixie put her leg on the desk to stretch.

"Trixie, go home. I'm tired."

Buck pushed her aside and left, angering Trixie. He decided he was probably the first man to cast her aside like some fish. Buck didn't care because he found her undesirable. He didn't realize Trixie decided to follow him. At his apartment, Buck got undressed and turned on the water for his bath. The phone rang distracting him from the woman sneaking into the apartment. She crept into the bathroom and got undressed. Buck grabbed his robe and answered the phone.

"Hello."

"Buck, how could you?"

"What?"

"A week to fix!" Angelique yelled.

"What are you talking about?"

"My plumbing. It's ruined."

"That's a shame."

"That's a shame? That's all you have to say?"

"What do you want me to say?"

"Why did you sabotage me?"

"Sabotage?" Buck asked.

"Yes. Files from your company found in the pipes, pipes deliberately broken, clogged system, and pipes wrenched to the point of bursting."

"I didn't do it."

"You had access and your name was on it. All my guests are out on the street. They won't come back. Many of them are from the retirement community too. Don't lie. I know you did it."

"You put the people out?"

"What was I supposed to do? I have no plumbing for a week."

"That was cruel, Angel."

"Don't call me that! You don't have the right. You don't love me. You just wanted to get in my inn to ruin me. I hate you."

Angelique slammed the phone. Buck noticed the water in the tub had stopped. *Someone is in my apartment*, he thought. Buck walked into the kitchen and opened a locked cabinet. He took out his nine millimeter and crept slowly into his bedroom. Buck did not like to use his gun, but sometimes, like now, he had no choice. He jumped into the bedroom but saw no one. He put the gun inside his robe and walked into the bathroom.

"Ack." Buck shouted when he saw Trixie playing with bubbles in his tub naked.

"Hello, Mr. Robertson. Come join me. The water is warm."

Buck raised his gun from his robes and aimed. He thought she was a disturbed woman.

"Trixie, you scared me. Why are you here?"

"Boy are you dumb! Can't you figure out why I'm here?"

"I don't want you here." For a moment, Buck thought he would take Trixie, but he came to his senses.

"I ain't leavin' until you come in the tub."

"No."

Trixie shrugged, left the tub and grabbed Buck's arm. She kissed his chest. Buck shoved the gun into her nose.

"What do you want really?"

Trixie shrugged again. She began to seduce Buck who was both aroused and angry at the same time. He cocked the gun.

"I asked you what you're doing here."

"Mr. Kennedy's orders. He says to break up you and that girl."

Trixie licked his belly button. Buck lowered the gun and lifted Trixie's head to look at her.

"Why does he want to do that?"

"Dunno. Didn't tell me. Didn't ask. I don't question when someone throws bills on the table. Why do you have a gun? Mr. Kennedy says you're his manager."

"That's right. This is a dangerous part of Philly. I need protection," Buck said. He was sure Trixie would accept the lie.

"Oh. If we don't do it, he'll hurt me probably. Anyway, I can see you're strong. I'd like to do it anyway."

"No, Trixie. We're not doing it. But feel free to tell Mr. Kennedy we did and that we broke up. Because after tonight's phone call, I doubt Angelique wants to talk to me again."

"But no man has ever refused me before. Look at my body. Tell me this isn't making your mouth water," she pleaded.

"It's nice. But I'm a gentleman and do not use women." Buck picked up her clothes from the floor and handed them to her.

"Get dressed." Buck walked to his living room and waited. *Why is Angelique so upset with him? Why is she accusing him? Why did Mr. Kennedy care about his love life? What was Mr. Kennedy doing with the ships?* Trixie kissed him as she passed.

"Thank you for being nice to me. Men aren't always nice."

"I could tell. Go home."

Trixie left but went to the bar instead of her home where she knew Mr. Kennedy waited. As soon as he saw her enter, he grabbed her.

"You do as I say?"

"Yeah. All done. The girl is so jealous. She'll never speak to him again." Mr. Kennedy grinned. They went into the back room, and Trixie pleasured him all night. They both needed it.

# Chapter 21
## *The Stalker*

Angelique knocked on Room 18. She could not stand still because she feared the mysterious guest in that room. She knew he would not be happy about leaving. Angelique wanted to get rid of him, but he paid for a month in advance in cash. Something about him made her nervous. He kept to himself, wore dark glasses to hide his eyes and walked with a limp. The large man liked to wear a long raincoat and baseball cap even on sunny days. He did not like to join the others for afternoon tea and festivities. At least, now she had an excuse to make him leave.

"I'm sorry sir, but we have to close for at least a week so we can fix our plumbing. You're welcome to return once the 1776 Inn reopens," she told the guest.

"I expect a refund for the week I'm not staying," he snapped and hid his sinister smile at the mention of plumbing.

"Of course. You'll also get a free night's stay you can use any time of the year."

"Thanks. Where can I go?"

"The Sheraton and Hilton hotels both have rooms."
"Yours is much more economical."

She trembled at his demeanor. She wondered if the man was a tourist. He did not act like one. She could not figure out why he would pay for a month in cash if he was not a tourist. She decided he must be eccentric, but he still scared her. Some days she considered that the man wanted to know all about her. She thought he might be the one stalking her and learning where she goes. She had no proof. She must be paranoid. She did not expect the man to go home and to follow her one last time. She did not know that he wanted to find out where she was going to stay during the plumbing repairs. The man grinned. She trembled again.

Despite her fear, she said in her professional voice, "I'm sorry. I have to fix the plumbing."

Before she moved to the next room, Angelique peaked in the man's room. The man quickly shut his door when he saw her glancing in his room. Angelique was glad to be at the next door. She heard him whip out his cell phone. The words he said were garbled. She leaned in closer to eavesdrop before she knocked on doors.

"Yes. It will be taken care of."

After hanging up, he dialed two men for the project. Everything was set. He just needed a location and a final plan.

# Chapter 22
## *The Shelter*

"Where should we go?" Angelique asked Maggie.

"Why don't we go to the hotel where ya are sendin' everyone else?"

"Because once I pay the difference between our price and the hotel, I won't have enough left to pay for us. Half of our guests were gratis anyway because of the fire." She began to cry.

"I'm going to lose my inn."

"Don't ya worry, Miss Angelique. God will help us." Maggie patted her back.

Angelique's tears lessened. "You're right, Maggie."

She could always count on Maggie to say the right things at the right time. Once, she had failed a major exam and was scared to tell her mother. Maggie told her to be honest and everything would work out right. Her mother hugged her and told her she would talk to the teacher. After the conversation with the teacher, Angelique was offered a tutor and brought up her grades. Maggie stood by her the whole time. The two friends sat in the inn's lounge, which was draped in flora prints from colonial days. They were trying to find a place to go. The rain tapped the windows.

"Why don't we go to Mr. Buck's place? He owes ya for puttin' up all his relatives."

"We're not going there! He put my inn to the brink of bankruptcy! He is just using me for his evil purposes."

"Ah don' think he did this. Ah think he's a good man. Why don't ya talk to 'im?"

"Never! I'm finished with him."

Before Maggie could argue with her more, Angelique ran out the door and headed toward Penn's Landing. She started to cry again. She did not know what to do. Worry and anxiety weighed on her, making each step take a long time.

"God, I need a shelter, a place to go. I need to save my inn. Please help me," she prayed.

She looked at the Delaware River Touring Co. ship on the river. Angelique's anger rose inside her and replaced her anxiety. She marched away from the touring company. As she walked she saw a sign: St. Vincent de Paul Society. She figured this was answer to her prayer. She had an idea. She walked over to the door and knocked. A nun wearing a light blue habit with a white shirt answered the door. Her curly brown hair hung
below the hat.

"May I help you?"

"Hello, Sister. My name is Angelique Chalfonte. I own the 1776 Inn. We had a problem with our plumbing. I put the guests up in a hotel but I can't afford to put up myself, my housekeeper and my cook in the hotel. I wonder if you could give us beds for a week."

"My dear, you look so troubled. Don't worry. Everything will get better. My name is Sister Maryanne. We have a few beds available but usually we offer them to the poor. It has been raining so much, and nights are still chilly."

"I understand, Sister Maryanne. I just don't know where else to go." Angelique's eyes filled with tears. "My parents died when I was in my teens. I have no sisters, brothers or cousins."

She started to cry again.

"My dear, everything is OK. Of course you can stay, but if people who really need the beds knock, you will have to allow them the space."

"Yes, Sister. When I earn more, I'll give you a large donation. We'll be back tonight."

Angelique walked back to the inn. She did not realize how far she had walked. She was tired. Her eyes stung from the tears. Her breathing was labored too. She had cramps in her side. She did not notice the man following or that he smiled. She was lost in her world that she could not know he made his plans. When Angelique looked behind her, he disappeared into the shadows and an area that was noisy from rain and traffic. She did not see him dial his phone or hear him inform his helper what to do and where to meet him. When she reached the inn, Angelique found Maggie waiting for her, worried.

"Where ya been?"

"Walking. Pack. We're going to stay in St. Vincent de Paul Society Shelter for the week."

"Oh."

"We'll get a cab and go over there."

"Are ya sure that will be all right?"

"I spoke with Sister Maryanne. She said it was fine as long as no one else needs the shelter."

"Ah don't know about this."

"Can you think of another place to go?"

"No, Miss."

"Don't worry. Everything will be OK," Angelique said despite her own trepidations.

"Well all right. Ah'll pack. Ah'll go tell Chuck."

"Good. I'll call the cab and pack."

# Chapter 23
## *The Accidents*

Angelique heard thunder. The rain sprayed the windows and pounded the pavement. She got nervous when she saw the heavy downpour.

"Come on Maggie, Chuck. We have to go."

"Miss Angelique, I forgot somethin'. I'll get another cab."

"OK."

Angelique and her cook entered the cab. She told the driver where to go. The driver started to go. Another car followed. The car drove slowly but stayed close. The cab stopped at a red light. The car behind it turned, drove one block, turned again and sat at the intersection where the cab was. The light turned green for the cab. The driver drove slowly over the wet pavement into the intersection. The dark car with the red light suddenly accelerated. The driver put his foot on the gas and sped through the red light. Crash! The car hit the cab with so much force that the cab skidded along the damp roads and slammed into a pole. Just as the cab driver opened his door, the car slammed into the driver knocking him 10 feet and killing him. Another car smacked into the cab from the other side.

Angelique was thrown forward but the seat belt knocked her back. She jerked her head and hit the side door. Blood gushed from her forehead. The cook did not put on his seat belt and landed in the front. Angelique could not tell if he was alive. She heard sirens blaring before she drifted into unconsciousness. The two cars disappeared before anyone could identify them. The drivers abandoned the cars as was the agreement.

* * *

Buck had to drive the tour this evening. His captain called and said he couldn't work. Roxy had booked a full tour. Buck could not lose the revenue, so he took the helm. The dark clouds and heavy rain made Buck uneasy about this night. He took his gun just in case. A mysterious passenger boarded the ship. Buck could not shake the feeling the man was up to no good because he wore dark sunglasses even though it was night and raining, dark jeans and a dark shirt. An umbrella covered his head and shielded his face. Buck saw him looked over the railing at the river even though it rained.

Several miles down river, the lights stopped working. Buck could see no landmarks, only black water. *I thought the electrician fixed those lights*, Buck thought. He checked his radio to call for help. The radio signal was jammed. Buck did not like the situation, but he wanted to allay the tourists' fears that nothing was wrong.

"Folks, don't panic. I'll go check out the problem," Buck said over the intercom.

The darkness of the river, the black clouds, rain and the dark interior made the trip to the fuse box difficult. He could barely see his own hand. Buck grappled his way toward the back. Someone stopped him.

"Excuse me, I need to get to the box."

"You're not going anywhere," the man growled in a whisper.

"What?"

"I have a gun pointed at your heart." Buck cringed. His own gun was at the helm. He needed both hands free to get to the box.

"Turn. Walk to the upper deck." Buck did not say a word.

He walked. He climbed the stairs to the top deck. Rain water flowed all over the deck, making the floor slippery. Buck slid across the floor, fell into a door and hit his head. The door opened to reveal bags with white powder. Buck knew what they were, but the man with the gun was his most pressing problem. The man pushed Buck when he tried to stand. Buck was wet and had a gash on his head. The push knocked him into the railing. He hit his arm. The pain shot through his body. Buck tried to stand again but was kicked in the abdomen and legs. As Buck stumbled, the man knocked him against the railing. He hit his head, knocking him unconscious. Buck slipped once more before falling in the water and hitting several rocks.

Trixie stripped her clothes and Mr. Kennedy's and worked his body. She threw the clothes on the floor. Trixie worked him all night as was the agreement. Mr. Kennedy arrived sometime after nine. He was supposed to be there at eight, but he was late. He forced Trixie to keep doing it despite her fatigue. He was coming around the bar more often these days, giving her only an hour or two for a break. She liked the money and knew he would hurt her if she wanted to stop before Mr. Kennedy was ready.

"I was here from 8 o'clock. Got that?" Trixie nodded.

At dawn, Mr. Kennedy grabbed his clothes and grinned. Everything was back the way it was supposed to be. He felt on top of the world again. Mr. Kennedy took care of his problem, had a woman he could control and was getting money again.
Trixie started putting on her clothes. Mr. Kennedy told her to wait. He wanted to stare at her some more. Mr. Kennedy enjoyed

her body and wished he did not have to leave. He touched her breasts. She took a breath. His touch was hard. She stood there and let him grab her breasts. He slid his hand down her belly and down her legs. Trixie thought Mr. Kennedy was going to ask for more. She did not want to give him more. Her body ached. She wanted sleep, but she did not say a word. She let him touch her even though she did not like his force. She wanted to get dressed. Mr. Kennedy sighed, took one last touch and left.

# Chapter 24
## *The Rescues*

Maggie screamed when her cab reached the accident site. She had recognized the person on the stretcher.

"That's me boss. That's me boss!"

"Please stand back, Miss," the police officer said.

"That's me boss," she said again.

"Please calm down, Miss," he said. "We'll talk to you in a minute."

Tears filled Maggie's eyes. "Is she…"

She couldn't finished the question.

"No, Miss. But she's in bad shape. What's her name?"

"Angelique…Chalfonte," Maggie choked. "She owns the 1776 Inn near the river."

"What about the other one?"

"He's our cook. His name is Chuck Pomadoro," Maggie said with frightened eyes.

"Does he have family? Does Miss Chalfonte?"

"Angelique does not have any family. I'm her closest friend. Chuck…has…a daughter. I…don't….know…where… she…lives. His…wife…died…a…year…ago," Maggie stammered. She cried some more.

"Everything will be OK," the police officer said. His eyes gave away his lie but Maggie did not notice. The police radio blared. "All units, a man has gone missing from Delaware River Touring Co. He never came back when the ship returned to dock, according to his assistant. Several passengers heard a splash. Police backup requested at Penn's Landing. Further details coming."

Maggie covered her mouth. She was sure that was Buck but thought against telling the police. She could be wrong. The ambulance took Angelique and Chuck to Thomas Jefferson University Hospital, the same hospital as Buck's father.

"Officer, I don' have a car. I must get to the hospital," Maggie said through tears. "The trains aren't running."

"We can't take you. We have to go to the dock. Another accident has occurred."

"I can take her." A kindly woman in her 50s came to the accident site. She wore a light blue and white habit. "My name is Sister Maryanne. You must know an Angelique Chalfonte. I was expecting her this evening. I heard the accident through the window. I heard you screaming."

"She's me boss. I was coming to see ya too," Maggie said. "I need to get to the hospital, Sister. Pray for Angelique, please.

She's all I have left. Me mom died several years ago. Me dad left when I was a baby."

"Of course, I'll pray. My car is over there." She pointed to a parking lot and walked her to the car.

"What will I do? First, the plumbin'. Now this. I can't run that inn alone."

"What is your name?" Sister Maryanne was trying to distract her from her worries.

"Maggie Carter," she answered.

They arrived at the hospital in a few minutes despite the closed roads because of the accident.

\* \* \*

The scuba divers stood ready to enter the water. The river churned as the rain continued. The black sky blocked all visibility. Swells on the river rocked the Coast Guard ship that appeared with search lights. The scuba divers boarded, and the ship left. Splash! Several divers entered the water. The search began for Buck. But the divers had trouble seeing. They continued to search using the lights the Coast Guard had given them, but they had not found Buck. They kept searching until one in the morning. At that point, the police divers decided the sky was too dark.

"We must wait until morning," said the police captain.

"It's supposed to be sunny."

"Captain, we might not find him alive if we wait," a diver said.

"I know, but what can we do?"

Buck awoke with a pounding headache, incredible soreness in his arm and throbbing pain in his legs. He realized he was deep in the river. His legs felt broken. He could barely move them. He could barely breathe. Buck began to swim, which hurt his arm more. His broken legs dragged behind him. He pushed toward the surface. He had to get there, but his legs ached, and his head bled. Slowly, Buck moved up toward the surface. At what seemed an hour later, he felt air. He knew he reached the surface, but he could not stay afloat for long with his broken legs. As he bobbed above and below the surface for what seemed an eternity, the Coast Guard lights caught the top of his head.

"Sir," said a lieutenant to his commanding officer. "Look at the water!" he said.

"That's a head!" the commander said. He blew a whistle, which got the attention of the police working crowd control. Police officers began pointing. The ship sped across the water to the bobbing head. Officers donned their suits again and jumped into the water. Two men grabbed the bobbing man and helped him up a ladder thrown into the water. Once on the ship, the officers sped toward Penn's Landing. On the pier, they put Buck into an ambulance, which hurried to the hospital. Buck had passed out when he was on the Coast Guard ship.

# Chapter 25
## *Critical Condition*

The hospital staff wheeled Angelique to the trauma unit because she was barely alive. They worked on her, put tubes in her lungs to inflate them, inserted a blood bag into her arm to replenish the loss of blood, gave her oxygen, hooked her to a heart monitor and tried to stop the internal bleeding. Maggie and Sister Maryanne paced outside the door wringing their hands. Hours passed so slowly that Maggie thought the clock had stopped. Just before dawn, the staff members stabilized her condition, but she remained critical. She was placed in the critical care unit. When the second ambulance arrived, the staff pushed the gurney to the emergency center and began to work on Buck. His condition was not as bad as Angelique's, but he had trouble breathing, ingesting a lot of water in his lungs. The nurses gave him oxygen, which revived him. They put splints on his legs and a sling on his arm. Buck opened his eyes to see nurses and doctors all around him. The agony in his legs and arm shot through him like a bullet.

"Ouch!" he yelled.

The hospital staff noticed he was awake.

"Mr. Robertson, your left leg is shattered in several places. You'll need surgery to fix it. Your right leg is fine except for a sprain and a large gash. We'll stitch you and put a brace on it to fix that. It should be usable in a week," said the doctor with salt and pepper hair and blue eyes.

"Your arm is just sprained. We'll give you some pain medication."

Buck nodded in understanding. He felt a bandage where the gash was. His head hurt from the lump.

"Please sign these forms so we can get moving on your leg. Lie down. You have to go into surgery." Buck signed the forms and sank into the pillows on the gurney. He was cold and shivered. A nurse put a blanket on him. The staff pushed the gurney down the hall to the operating room door, gave Buck anesthesia and began operating on his leg.

Before he sank into unconsciousness, Buck thought he heard a nurse say in the distance, "When you finish here, they need you in the trauma center for Miss Chalfonte." *Angel is hurt. Wonder what happened*, Buck thought as he fell asleep.

Hours later, Buck lay on his hospital bed with a police officer in the room. His room was divided by a curtain. Heart monitors were on him, and equipment filled the room.

"Mr. Robertson, can you tell me what happened last night?" asked the officer.

"The ship lights went out. I went to find the fuse box. Someone attacked me and pushed me overboard. I think it was to look like an accident," Buck replied.

"Why?"

"I don't know, but it must have something to do with the

drugs I found on the ship."

"What drugs?"

"The FBI has suspected the ship's owner of smuggling and embezzlement for months now, but it couldn't get any evidence."

"How do you know that?" the police officer growled.

"I'm an undercover agent trying to get the evidence it needs. You can't blow my cover."

"Right. We need to pretend you died in that accident." "Do you know what happened to Angelique Chalfonte? Is she here?"

"Why would you ask that?" He sighed, then said, "Last night was a busy night. We are investigating a traffic accident involving her cab. Her cook and the cab driver died. Miss Chalfonte is in critical condition. Oh and your father is being released this morning. We'll bring him to your apartment."

"Was the accident deliberate?"

"We're investigating all possibilities, but we are leaning that way. We found the car that hit her. It was ditched on the Blue Route. We found folders and evidence in the trunk. We now don't think the two arsons, her accident and your attack are coincidences. We think they might be related. We are trying to find the owner of the car. The rain washed away a lot of evidence from the accident site. Do you think the things that have happened lately have something to do with what you are trying to find out?"

"Maybe. Angelique's inn also was deliberately damaged. The plumbing was destroyed. I heard that a large sum of money disappeared from her too."

"She never reported those things."

"She did not have time to report the plumbing damage. I don't know why she didn't report the theft. Maybe, she wanted to handle it on her own."

"Well, we'll look into it. I will tell the staff that you are not to have visitors and to pretend that Buck Robertson is dead."

"You might have to protect Angelique too."

"We can't. We don't know for sure that the accident was anything but someone running a red light. Therefore, we can't put extra manpower on it. I can tell the staff to limit her visitors too."

To change the subject he said, "I'm glad my father is doing better." He closed his eyes.

The police officer thought Buck needed sleep and left the room. He just wanted to think. He was worried about Angelique, but he would not be allowed to see her. The last time he talked to her, she blamed him for her troubles at the inn. *Even if the hospital let me visit, Angelique will not want me around. If she is so critical, she will not know I'm there anyway. Would Maggie let me see her or does she believe I'm guilty too?*

Maggie and Sister Maryanne stood at a vigil by Angelique's side. Dried tears dotted Maggie's eyes. Sister Maryanne held her hand the whole time. She was concerned. They prayed a rosary together. In the late morning, they received a visitor.

"Miss Carter?" a young police officer with blonde hair called. His uniform was perfectly pressed. Maggie looked at her own clothes, which were disheveled. Her floral print dress was covered with a dirty apron. Mud was flung in her hair.

"Yeah?" Maggie asked.

"I am Officer Bellows. Are you up to answering a few questions?" he asked gruffly.

"Ah guess so." Maggie shrugged.

"What do you remember about last night?"

"We was supposed to get in the cab together, but Ah forgot to pack somethin'. Me suitcase is old and wouldn't lock so Ah had to hunt for a way ta keep it locked. Ah told Miss Angelique Ah'd get another cab. Ah left about an hour later."

"How long you been working for Miss Chalfonte?"

"We grew up together. Me mum was her nanny when her parents were alive. Me mum died from heart attack a few years ago."

"Go on with your story."

"Well, Ah arrived at the scene and saw them tending to her. Ah started screaming."

"Did you see how it happened?"

"No sir. The accident was over when Ah got there."

"Anything else unusual happen?"

"Well, Miss Angelique's inn was damaged. Someone ruined her plumbing. It will take a week to fix. Miss Angelique blames Mr. Robertson, but Ah don' think so. And, some weird guy paid for a whole month in cash. Ah don' know his name. That was not my job. He made Angelique nervous."

"Mr. Robertson?" the police officer asked incredulously.

"Yeah, 'im. He seems too nice to do this."

"Do you know he fell overboard last night and is in this hospital with a shattered leg and a torn ligament? He nearly drowned."

"In this hospital?"

"That's right."

"Interesting'," was all she could say. The information shocked her too much. "Do you think they're related?"

"The people?"

"No sir. The accidents."

"We're investigating every possibility. The captain decided that until we know for sure if Miss Chalfonte's life is in danger you are not to let anyone visit her room."

"Miss Angelique's life might be in danger?"

"We don't know. It's one possibility. Until we know for sure, we want her to be safe."

"Yes, sir. Ah'll make sure she's safe."

"Well, I better go."

Sister Maryanne and Maggie resumed their vigil. The accidents were a coincidence, she was sure. The news about Angelique's life being in danger worried her but she discounted it. *Who would hurt her?* Still, she would do anything for her. The inn would remain closed until Angelique was better, Maggie said. Soon, exhaustion got the better of Sister Maryanne and Maggie, and they dozed.

# Chapter 26
## *Secret Visit*

Buck was determined to see Angelique even if he could only glance at her. He wished he could tell her the truth, but he is not allowed. Someone is trying to frame him and disgrace him in her eyes. He hated seeing her so sad, frightened and worried. But even angry, her eyes burned with love for him. He could tell. The thought of her barely alive was too much to take. He also knew he had to talk with her. The events were connected, but he had to figure out how. Buck decided he could visit her after midnight. He knew only a handful of workers are in hospitals overnight. He would arouse less suspicion then. His legs were still too weak for any weight. He needed a wheel chair, but he would have to ask the hospital staff for a chair. The nurse would not let him go, he decided, but he could at least ask. *Just in case she says no, I must find another way.*

He scanned his room. He saw a janitor left a mop in the corner. The elderly man in the next bed threw up overnight. Buck hobbled over to the mop and stumbled a few times before reaching it. He unscrewed the mop head and fashioned it under his arm. It was not the best, but he was able to stand fairly well on his less injured leg. The pain was unbearable, but he ignored it.

Stumbling back to his bed, he slipped the makeshift cane under his blankets. After midnight, he would try to see her. The nurse wearing bright-colored scrubs entered to record his vitals.

"How are you?"

"Getting to the bathroom is difficult," Buck said. "A chair would be easier for me."

"Mr. Robertson, you know you are supposed to be assisted to the bathroom."

"Yes, I know. I just thought I could do it myself if I had a wheelchair."

"Sorry. You're not allowed."

"Where is the trauma center?"

"Why do you want to know?"

"The police officer told me a woman came here last night and was put there. I was just curious where it was," Buck said matter-of-factly. He shrugged to make his curiosity seem more real.

"It's on the fourth floor, but the woman is now in the critical care unit. That's on the fifth floor."

"Thanks."

After the hospital got quiet, and the nurse had recorded his vitals for the night, Buck took the mop handle, removed his monitors and slowly worked his way to the elevator. He carefully watched his surroundings to make sure no one saw him. Besides the hospital staff, Buck did not want whomever attacked him to know he was alive. He pushed the button hard, willing the elevator to come in a hurry. The pain in his legs made his eyes water. Buck found the critical care unit and as quietly as possible entered because he didn't want to wake Maggie who slept

in a chair outside the room. Angelique began to stir. Buck thanked God that she would live. Their prayers were answered. Then, he looked at the purple-bruised face of
Angelique and the tubes in her arms and face. He cried but not from pain.

"I'm so sorry, my Angel. You would not be in this mess if you had never met me. I wish I could make everything right for you."

Angelique heard him although Buck had no idea she had. She moaned.

"I have to find the person who did this to you! I want us to be together. That is if you don't hate me." Buck sobbed.

"Buck?" Angelique whispered in a scratchy tone.

Buck jumped. He was not expecting her to say anything. Angelique looked at him. She could see he was hurt too.

"What happened?"

"You were in a car accident, but the hospital is taking care of you."

"No. To you," she squeaked.

"Me? I'm all right."

But his face revealed his searing pain.

"No. You're hurt. You need to rest. Why see me?"

"I...uh... I don't know. I had to see you. I'll go back to my room."

"No. Stay. I want…" Angelique could not finish her sentence.

"Angel, I know you don't believe me, but I had nothing to do with the sabotage at your inn or your accident. I…" Buck hesitated then added, "love you too much."

"I know, Buck. You are hurt. You wouldn't be here if you didn't love me. Do you know who did?" she sputtered.

"No, but it must be related to the strange happenings at the touring company."

Buck put all his weight on the mop handle, leaned over her, smiled and kissed her forehead. "Don't worry, my Darling. I will find out. I must get back to my room now. I probably won't come back."

"I love you too, Buck," Angelique whispered before falling into a deep sleep again. Buck hobbled back to his room, careful to avoid people. Once he crept back to his bed, he rang the nurse to complain about the pain in his legs. When she left, Buck stayed awake awhile and thought about the events over the last few weeks. *I must be close to the truth if they are trying to kill me.*

# Chapter 27
## *Maggie's Assignment*

A pile of money laid on the table between two men, Mr. Kennedy and the man in the trench coat.

"Deed done?" growled Kennedy.

"Yes. No one will know the deaths weren't accidents."

"My problems gone for good?"

"Yes."

"Good. Take your pay and disappear. I don't want to be linked to you."

"Right." The man left the pool hall and headed South on I-95 toward the airport. The passport he had stolen would come in handy. The man's helpers would leave by train, one heading north, the other west. At the airport parking lot, the man passed the two helpers and gave them their cut. All three were gone quickly. All of them looked back at Philadelphia once before leaving the city forever.

Buck went home a few days later. His father helped him at home because he could not walk well. The hospital provided a wheel chair and crutches. He checked before leaving and learned Angelique was moved from the critical care unit to a regular room. Buck desperately wanted to talk to her about what happened and to see her, but his father wouldn't hear of it.

"You are much too weak to travel back and forth to the hospital. Besides you have work to do. Have you figured out who set the fire yet?"

"The fire at the retirement home? I'm not working on that case. The local police are."

"Well, it must be connected. It's too much of a coincidence."

"The police thinks so too, especially with what happened to me and Angelique." Buck sat silently.

He decided to visit the retirement community, which was letting people back into some of the less damaged apartments, to see what he could find out from friends. The problem was getting there with his bad legs.

* * *

Angelique improved. The tubes were removed except for an intravenous drip of pain medicine. The bruises on her face turned a brownish green with rings of yellow. Her head remained bandaged. She could eat light foods. Maggie did not have the heart to tell her about Chuck. His daughter claimed the body and held a small funeral. Maggie attended the viewing and Mass. Maggie also let the plumber in the inn. He was nearly finished. The rest of the time Maggie sat by Angelique's bedside.

"Maggie, do you know what happened?" Angelique asked.

"Ah didn't see the accident, just afterwards."

"I don't think it was an accident," she said matter-of-factly. "I remember the car speeding through the red light. I'm quite sure he followed the cab too. And, a second car hit me."
"Ya need to tell the police this."

"The nurses will not let me use the telephone. They don't want me to get excited. My heart is not ready for that, they tell me."

Maggie nodded. "The police are lookin' at every possibility."

"So Buck was behind this too."

"Ah don't think so. Ah think he's a good man."

"Maybe. I'm not sure, but I think I had a dream where he was talking to me. He told me it was related to strange goings-on at the pier. He was hurt too. But what makes you so sure he's not involved? He does work at that touring company."

"The police is worried about ya. They think you're in danger. They still investigatin'. They have no leads," Maggie said.

"That's why we have to do our own investigating."

"Miss Angelique, ya too hurt to go around town stirring up trouble, and Ah don't want ya in more danger."

"You are going to do it. Talk to Roxy and some of the men. See what you can find out."

Maggie stood like a statue. Her fear rooted her to the spot sending shivers down her spine. "Me? I no investigator."

"Maggie, it has to be you. No one is better at spreading gossip. No one at the Delaware River Touring Co. knows you either. You can pretend to buy tickets or something. I don't want Mr. Kennedy to know I survived the crash."

"What are ya goin' to do?"

"The morning nurse told the police captain that I was well enough to answer questions in person. The captain plans to stop by later. I'll tell him what I know then."

"Then ya don' need me to investigate."

"Maggie, I only know about the accident. I don't know about other things that might have an impact. All this also is hurting my inn. I have to save my inn."

"Miss Angelique, the police said ya life might be in danger and to protect ya. What if Ah ask questions and then my life is in danger?"

"I know you are scared, but I know you can do it. If Mr. Kennedy does not know who you are, you won't be put in danger. But if he is there, please do not investigate. Come back to the inn. OK?"

"Who will protect ya while Ah'm not here?"

"The police told the hospital staff to limit my visitors. The staff will protect me."

"Well, Ah guess Ah can talk to the men," she said reluctantly.

Angelique smiled because Maggie recognized she was right. She had to find out the truth to protect the inn. Maggie left the hospital room and headed for Penn's Landing.

# Chapter 28
## *Roxy's Thoughts*

Roxy looked ragged. She had her job and some of Buck's job. She worked 14-hour days since Buck's disappearance. Mr. Kennedy visited her several times a day to make sure she worked. He knew he had to hire a new manager but did not want Roxy to know that he knew Buck was dead. Roxy kept asking whether a new manager was coming or whether Mr. Robertson was found. Mr. Kennedy ignored Roxy most of the time and told her to just keep booking tours.

"We are keeping his job available in case he's found," Kennedy told her. "Just get the tours and profits. Don't worry about the books. I'll handle those."

"But sir. The men haven't been paid. I don't know how to do that."

"Tell them they'll get their check!"

"Two of the men have not come back to work."

"Fire them. Tell the rest to pick up the slack. I can't afford to hire anyone else!"

Mr. Kennedy paused to compose himself and added, "I need the boat for a private party on Saturdays for the next two months."

"That's our best tour day. We'll lose…"

"Who is the owner? Me or you? Do as I say!" Mr. Kennedy barked at her and abruptly left.

"Yes, sir," she said but she cracked a large bubble of her gum as he left. After the door closed, Roxy made a face and stuck out her tongue. Unfortunately for Roxy, that is when Maggie entered.

"May I help you?" Roxy said eyeing her suspiciously.

"Yessim. I am a friend to Miss Chalfonte. Ya remember her. She worked here for a week?"

Roxy smiled. She liked Miss Chalfonte a lot. She liked how happy she made Mr. Robertson. "Of course. What can I do for you?"

"Well, strange things are happenin' at the inn. Miss Chalfonte thinks they might be linked to strange things happenin' here."

Roxy blew a bubble. "I'll say. Strange stuff is going on here. I didn't think so until Mr. Robertson never came back from the boat a week ago. I told the police he never piloted the boat and always was diligent about recording everything. He never would have gone and not come back without my knowing about it."

"Ya said strange stuff?"

"Yeah. The captain that was supposed to pilot the boat

called out sick and hasn't returned. Two men left. They had been here for years, but they didn't even give notice. Mr. Kennedy wants more private tours and this is a guy who is always concerned for profits. I heard Mr. Robertson talkin' in code. I don't think Mr. Robertson is involved in these strange things. He is much too nice. I hope he gets together with Miss Chalfonte. He loves her too much. You should of seen him mope when she wasn't talking to him."

"Yes. I seen that too. They don't want to admit. But I know they'll end up together."

"Is Mr. Robertson alive?"

"I don't know. I assumed he is."

"The police said they could not find his body and suspect he died."

"Really? They could not find his body?"

Roxy nodded. Maggie was startled. She was sure the police officer told her he was in the hospital when Angelique was.

She tried not to show her surprise and asked, "What else can ya tell me?"

"Well I overheard a fight between Mr. Kennedy and Enrique Bañal, one of the missing men. Enrique wanted payment for something and wanted Mr. Kennedy to do something for his sister Rosetta who has all these kids. At least, I think he meant kids. He said 'charges.'"

"Indeed," was all Maggie could say.

"I'm up to my eyeballs in work. If Mr. Robertson is alive, tell him to come back," Roxy pleaded.

"Mr. Robertson's not talkin' to Miss Chalfonte. I doubt I will see 'im."

"Darn. What's been happening at the inn?" Roxy asked. She was always keen on hearing gossip.

"Miss Chalfonte's plumbin' ruined. She had to put her guests in a hotel. Funds are missing. Her sales are down, partly 'cuz she told off Mr. Kennedy. She's also done a lot of charity with the fire and Mr. Robertson's relatives. She had a fire. And, she was in a terrible car accident. She almost died."

"That's too bad. Miss Chalfonte is nice."

"Then of course the medical bills will eat away at more profits."

"Medical bills?"

"The bills from the hospital where she has been since the accident. She has been there for a week already. She has no insurance."

"A week? That's the night Mr. Robertson never came back from the boat. I wonder." She blew another bubble.

"Listen, Roxy, I better go. Miss Chalfonte needs me and ya are loaded with work."

"Yeah. It was nice talkin' to ya."

"Whatever ya do, don' tell Mr. Kennedy, we talked."

"I don't even like talking to him when I have to talk to him. He'll never know."

"Don' tell him about Miss Angelique either."

"Fine."

Maggie started to leave and added, "By the way, I know the

face was not for me." Roxy blushed and looked at her papers. Maggie smiled and walked out the door.

# Chapter 29
## *Mrs. Mateo's Gossip*

Buck did his own investigating. He visited Mrs. Mateo at the apartment building and met her sister as well.

"Hi, Mrs. Mateo. Hello, Mrs. O'Reilly."

"Well look what the cat dragged in," said Mrs. Mateo surprised.

"How ya doin'? That funeral was a beautiful service," Mrs. O'Reilly said. Mrs. Mateo nodded.

"Thanks. I'm doing fine, but I'll be on these crutches for a few weeks. Accident at work," he quickly added to avoid questions about it.

"Didja eat?" I have chicken."

"Chicken sounds great."

"Have a seat."

"I'd love some too, Sis."

Mrs. Mateo fumbled in the kitchen for a few minutes and returned with a platter of chicken and plates.

"What can I do for you?" Mrs. Mateo asked as she placed the chicken on a plate and handed it to Buck.

"I thought I'd stop by and enjoy your company. Dad's out the hospital. He's at my place. I can't work and I'm bored. Dad's starting to drive me crazy," lied Buck.

"Tsk-Tsk. Such a horrible thing that fire. So many lives lost," Mrs. O'Reilly said.

"I agree. The papers say the police still don't have leads, but a friend in the force said an anonymous tip is pointing toward a connection to other things," Mrs. Mateo said.

"What other things?"

"Well break-in at the 1776 Inn for one. My sister heard the burglar. A few days later, she said she had to leave because the plumbing wasn't working. She told that nice detective who is handling the arson case."

"Yeah," said Mrs. O'Reilly. "That's not all. I heard some of the guests talking about removing a nosy manager and his slutty girlfriend. Well it has to be Mr. Aikens at the retirement community and that Trixie woman. They never care about us. She's always in his office for hours. Forgot all about the faulty wiring we had complained about one day she was there. I insisted he at least tell the owner.

Buck froze and sat straight in his seat. He knew Trixie. *How can she be involved?* he thought. *Was the manager me?*

"Who owns the retirement community?"

"Some guy named Mr. Kennedy. He's never there but always collects his rent."

Buck felt icy water drip down his back. He held his crutches tight. *What was he up to?* Buck thought.

"Do the police suspect Kennedy for the arson?"

"Not that I heard. My friend said he was out of town for two weeks when it happened," said Mrs. Mateo. "They are trying to get him for being a slum landlord."

Buck remembered he hadn't seen Kennedy at the touring company during that time. *He did it. But how do I prove it?*

"Do you know if he had an insurance policy on the retirement community?"

"Oh yeah, he did. Something like $50 million, but the insurance company won't pay on account of the arson investigation," Mrs. O'Reilly said.

"Thank you for the chicken. It was delicious. I better leave. My legs are starting to hurt and Dad has been alone for too long." The ladies nodded and showed Buck the door.

# Chapter 30
*Pieces of the Puzzle*

Maggie heard sobs coming from Angelique's hospital room.

"Miss Angelique, don't worry. We'll get the inn running again."

"What? The inn? Right. I'm worried about the bills. That's it," Angelique said hurriedly.

She wanted to conceal the reason for the tears.

"Ya not heard about Chuck, then?"

"Chuck? Why? Is he all right?"

"He died, Miss. He died the night of the car crash. Right here in the hospital. Ya got no cook."

"Oh dear. No I hadn't heard. One more thing to send me for bankruptcy. I might as well file now."

"Miss Angelique, don' say stuff like that. We've always pulled through before. We'll pull through again."

"Yeah. I guess so."

"Miss, if ya weren't crying over the inn or Chuck, what was it?"

"Nothing. I just feel overwhelmed and lonely. I want to go home." That was only partly true.

"Ya be home in a couple of days. Doc said so."

"Yeah."

Angelique wiped her face from the straggling tears and lay silent for awhile. She wanted to change the subject. She did not want Maggie to know that she cried over Buck. He hadn't come to see her. He must have heard about the crash. He must be worried, but the last time Angelique spoke to him, she told him to never to speak to her again. He must have listened. She sobbed because of the mistake she made. She did not remember the night in the hospital room. She assumed it was a dream. Maggie was asleep that night and did not know about it either. Maggie gazed at her boss lying on the bed still with bruises all over her and decided to tell her what Roxy said.

"Did you say charges?"

"Yes. Roxy said 'charges'. She thought he meant kids."

"That explains it."

"That explains what?"

"Never mind. I just remembered something. Did you say Buck disappeared the night of my car accident?"

"Yes. Roxy hasn't seen 'im. The police are investigatin' but haven't told her nothin'.""

Angelique could tell Maggie was hiding something but didn't pursue the conversation. She sensed it wouldn't be wise to push her for information she might not want to know.

"He's in danger. I have to warn him."

"How? Ya in here and don' know where he is."

"His father knows. I'll call him."

"His father was released."

"Where's he staying? The retirement community is not rebuilt."

"Don' know. Mr. Buck's?"

"Yes. He would be there."

A nurse entered to record her vitals. She told Angelique to take medicine to put her to sleep. "You need to rest."

"But I don't want to rest."

"Do you want to be released soon? You must rest."

She drifted asleep.

Buck told his dad what he heard from the women and his opinion that Kennedy had something to do with the fire.

"How do I prove it?"

"Son, you are one of the best agents. You will figure out a way."

"I need to get Kennedy's men to talk. One of them will give up Kennedy, I'm sure of it. I found a gun and files when I searched their lockers."

"How are you going to interrogate them when you are on crutches and supposed to be dead?"

Buck laughed. "I guess I'm not too intimidating on these. Also, to protect my cover, I can't go back. I have to let Kennedy think I drowned."

"Isn't there anyone you can ask for help? Someone you trust?"

"I trust Angelique, but she is in no condition. I don't think her accident was an accident. I think she is in danger herself."

"Why? She's a bed and breakfast owner."

"I think she knows too much but doesn't realize what she knows. That might be why he set the fire—to get rid of someone who knows too much. Wait a minute," Buck said excitedly.

"What son?"

"Mrs. O'Reilly complained about Trixie and Mr. Aikens. I know Trixie is a highly paid hooker that had to seduce me because Mr. Kennedy told her. What if she seduced Aikens to do his work for him?"

Stanley shook his head. "Mr. Aikens is dead. The fire started in his apartment. The firefighters couldn't get him out in time," Stanley added.

"What?" Buck said surprised. "That's the one who knew too much! He must have heard it from Trixie!"

"I think you're right son."

"I have to warn Angelique. If Kennedy finds out she's alive…" His voice trailed off.

"Son, you can't go. You'll get hurt. He's after you too. I already lost my wife. I can't lose you too."

"I know Dad. I know. I can't call her. My phone might be bugged."

"How about a letter? He can't inspect the mail."

"I don't know how to explain all this in a letter besides she doesn't know the truth."

Buck slumped in his chair worrying about Angelique and wondering how to prove his conclusions.

# Chapter 31
## *The Mailing*

In the two-bedroom apartment near Washington Square, Buck paced the shaggy blue rug in his living room, over and over, which made his legs take longer to heal. His dad told him to stop. He couldn't help himself. Buck agonized over Angelique. He feared she was dead, wondered how to contact her without Mr. Kennedy finding out, worried about not getting the proof he needed while his leg was injured and worried about how Roxy was doing at the company. He did not dare use his phone in case it was bugged. His dad also wanted him to lay low. Buck did send a message to his department for instructions. His boss agreed that further investigation might put everyone in danger and blow his cover. Further contact also might make Kennedy get scared and dispose of any evidence. The department worked with the local police to build a case. Buck had given his boss his theories. Every time he rehashed the issues in his mind, he failed to come up with solutions.

Angelique's body healed as the weeks passed, but her heart broke more and more. She had not heard from Buck and decided against calling his father. *If he does not want to find me, I'm not going looking for him*, she thought. He can protect himself. She stayed in her room and worked out ways to promote her inn, which helped her get her mind off Buck. But at bed time, Angelique sobbed from loneliness. The rainy days did not help improve her mood.

Over the weeks, it rained nearly three times a week. She prayed for help with the inn. But as the days passed, no help came. Angelique struggled to keep guests. Word had spread that her inn's plumbing could flood easily and was unsanitary. Angelique had to cook the breakfasts and muffins for afternoon tea because she could not afford to hire a new cook. She felt she had to fire Maggie but could not do it. Maggie was too much of a friend. She asked her to take a pay cut. Angelique cut corners else where to make up the difference. She used plain tea instead of fancy flavors, did not offer lemons anymore or cream, switched to one-ply toilet paper and washed linens only once-a-week instead of every day. *If business does not pick up soon, I might have to close for good.* That realization lowered her spirits even further. This was her parents' dream. She decided to do a mass mailing of promotional letters. She got them ready for mailing but needed stamps.

"I'm going to the Post Office," she told Maggie.

"Ya think that's wise?"

"I have to mail these letters or we have to close. I won't live as a prisoner in my home."

"Yeah, OK. I can go for ya."

"You're already doing enough. Nothing has happened to me in weeks. I'll be fine."

"That's because you haven't left the inn. Please be careful."

"I will."

Angelique got to the Post Office and stood in line. She gasped. Two people ahead of her stood Mr. Kennedy. *He doesn't know I'm here. It will be OK.* She took a deep breath. But her hands were dripping in sweat. Her heart pounded in her chest. Mr.

Kennedy dropped his package he carried. The paper ripped at one end. Angelique noticed a bag of white powder. She quickly looked away. She did not want Mr. Kennedy to see her. But Mr. Kennedy had seen her when he bent to pick up his package. After he mailed his package, he walked to Angelique. He tried to be polite without showing his surprise at seeing her alive.

"Hello, Miss Chalfonte."

"Hello, Mr. Kennedy," Angelique said in a shaky voice trying to stay calm.

"You look well. How's business?"

"I'm fine. The inn is doing all right," she said, trying to sound casual. She did not want him to know her problems. She covered the letters she held tightly so he would not see what they were.

"I see." He whispered in her ear, "I'd be careful if I were you. Someone might try to kill you."

He marched out the door. Angelique froze in her spot. Not until a postal clerk said, "Ma'am you're holding up the line" did she move.

"Yes. I'm sorry. I need 100 stamps."

"Here you go."

Angelique left the Post Office definitely shaking. She stood at the curb wondering what she should do. She was scared. Her problems at the inn seemed small now. She decided to go to Buck's apartment. Even if he isn't there, his father will know where to find him. She found the address through the computer. She took the El to Buck's apartment and knocked. She was shocked when Buck opened the door using a cane.

# Chapter 32
## *Confiding in Buck*

"Angelique!" Buck shouted with delight. Then he frowned when he saw how much she shook. "What's wrong?"

"Buck, I'm surprised to find you here, but I'm so glad to see you."

"What's wrong?" he asked again.

"I…was…at the….Post Office…and saw….Franklin…. Kennedy…there."

Buck winced. He knew what it meant. Kennedy realized she survived.

"What did he say?"

"He told me that someone wants to kill me," she said calming herself. She started to cry.

Buck hugged Angelique. "It's all right. Everything will work out. I'm here for you."

Buck guided Angelique to the couch and put her down on it. Buck's father sat in a chair.

"I've been worried about you, but I was afraid to call you. I wasn't sure if you wanted to speak to me," Buck said.
Angelique realized for the first time that Buck was hurt.

"What happened to you?"she asked with worried eyes.

"I had an accident at work."

It was partly true. He did not have the heart to tell her the whole truth that someone tried kill them both on the same night, but Angelique suspected something else.

Seeing her face, he added, "Didn't you know I was hurt after I visited you in the hospital?"

"You never visited me. In fact, I don't know why I'm here. I could have died and you wouldn't care."

"I care a lot. I had to fashion myself a crutch from a mop handle and walk on searing pain while avoiding hospital staff just to see you in the critical care unit. You were awake. You knew I was there. I told you I would find who did this to you and that I love you," Buck defended.

"I thought that was a dream. I was heavily medicated."

"I couldn't see you after that. I couldn't risk a nurse finding me. I've been on crutches or in a wheel chair since I came home. Today, I got my cane. It was too difficult to take the El to you. So I stayed here and worried."

"Buck, were you hurt the same night I was?"

"Yes, I think."

"That's what Roxy said. I've had Maggie do some investigating for me. I'm sure it's not a coincidence that both of us were hurt the same night."

"I agree. It's not a coincidence."

Buck frowned at knowing that Angelique was putting herself in more danger by doing investigating on her own. Angelique proceeded to tell Buck everything Roxy said and her revelation on the knocking.

"That's why he wants to kill me. I know too much. And, on top of that, I saw a package with white powder inside the wrapping. My guess is anthrax and some terrorist's plot."

"No Angelique. Not anthrax, just heroine and cocaine. Franklin Kennedy is smuggling drugs on his boats. He must have mailed it to get rid of the evidence."

Buck told her what he concluded about Kennedy and the fires.

"Wow. That's why you're in danger. You're a witness to his awful deeds."

"Not all of them. You know about some of them."

"How can we prove it?"

"The only way is to catch him in the act of smuggling. Ask Roxy when the next 'private booking' is scheduled. We'll sneak aboard and hide before he arrives."

"That sounds dangerous."

"Don't worry. We won't be alone."

But he could not elaborate.

"I…don't want…to go…on the ship," she said frightened.

"Don't worry," Buck said again. "I won't let Kennedy do anything to you."

"No. Not Kennedy. I…have…" She took a deep breath and said, "not been on the water since my father died in that rescue attempt. The water scares me."

She told Buck about her father dying in a rescue attempt. She told him how her mother died not long after that from pneumonia from the same storm. She told him about seeing a little boy stuck in the water trying to get help and how her mother would not let her explain what she saw. She told him how these incidents made her hate water.

"What little boy? When was this? How old was he?"

"It was summer. I was about 4 so I guess he was around 8. Why?"

"That was me. We were visiting Philadelphia for Fourth of July. I slipped on a wet surface and fell in the river. I saw you and asked for help. A police officer came a few minutes after you left. I wasn't drowning. I knew how to swim but my foot was hurt."

"You were the boy? I guess we were supposed to meet."

"Yes. Angel, I can't protect you unless you're with me. But I understand what a parent's death can do to a person and would perfectly understand if you stayed at the inn."

"The inn!"

She shouted in revelation. Buck jumped and dropped his cane. He bent to get it.

"That bastard is behind the sabotage. He framed you using

the men who left. I will not let him ruin my parents life dream because of a fear of boats or water! I will see you on that boat!"

"I love you, Angel!"

"Oh Buck."

She kissed him. A warm sensation filled every inch of her body down to her toes. She felt safe. She felt like he would do anything for her.

"When you find out when the trip is, don't call me. Write me a note with these words: 'Early bird catches worm at and put the time without p.m. or a.m.' It would have to be night. Leave it at the mailbox for the retirement community. My father checks his mail daily. Most of the residents still get their checks and bills. Stay at the inn until the voyage. I want you safe."

"OK Buck. Be careful. He's after you too."

"I know. I will be."

# Chapter 33
## *The Deadly River*

Angelique phoned Roxy and found out the next private ship left at 11 o'clock that evening. She wrote her note to Buck and addressed it to Stanley as planned and put it in the mailbox of the retirement community. He had not yet gotten his mail that day. Angelique watched from her window. She breathed a sigh of relief when Stanley picked up the letter. Buck will get it, she thought.

"Maggie you will need to tend to the guests tonight. I have something to do," Angelique said.

"Ya not doin' more investigatin' are ya?"

"Yes, I am. I'm going on the river."

"Ya'll put yourself in danger."

"Just tend to the guests. I'll take care of myself."

"Fine, Miss Angelique. We only have three rooms booked anyhow."

Angelique shed a tear at this news but turned from Maggie.

She went to her room and looked in her closet for something inconspicuous to wear. She pulled out dark denim pants, a navy polo shirt and a Phillies baseball cap. She glanced at the clock. She still had four hours to kill. She sat at her desk to do the accounting. She stared out the window. It rained again although intermittently. She had a message on her desk from a reporter of *Philadelphia Magazine*. She dialed the number. The reporter wanted to feature her inn. Angelique answered all her questions. She then told the reporter about illegal drugs, illegal immigrants and strange disappearances at the Delaware River Touring Co.

"We're going to get proof tonight. Be at the pier around midnight. You'll have your proof and a cover story exclusive to your magazine. All I ask is that you feature my inn prominently and positively," Angelique said.

"Thanks for the tip, Angelique. There will be no problem featuring your inn prominently. I hope business picks up for you and your troubles subside."

"I hope so too. Thanks for the feature on my inn. Bye."

"No problem."

At 10:30 p.m., Angelique changed into her clothes and descended her stairs to the foyer. The rain came down harder now. Lightning flashed. Thunder crashed. She held the knob of her front door about to turn it when it burst open. Mr. Kennedy stood in her doorway with a gun pointed at her chest.

"You're coming with me. Get moving."

"Why would I go with you?"

"Shut up and walk! You are my insurance policy."

He grabbed her arm so tightly her fingers turned blue from lack of blood circulation. She stumbled down the steps.

*  *  *

Meanwhile, Buck called Roxy to book passage. He disguised his voice and used a different name. He got a ticket for his wife too. Buck knew that Roxy did not care who the passengers were. He looked for a disguise. He wore a wig of white and put on a white mustache. He found shabby clothes and put them on his body. The cane went well with his disguise. Right before he left, Buck grabbed his gun, which the police had returned to him once they tested it.

"Be careful, Son," Buck's father said.

"I will, Dad. Don't worry. You won't lose a son. It's all part of the job."

"I know that, but the job is dangerous. You are all I have."

"I love you, Dad."

"Love you too, Son."

Buck left and boarded the boat. Black clouds covered the sky. The rain came down in sheets. He saw Mr. Kennedy gripping Angelique. He recognized her from her hair, eyes and curves despite her attempts to disguise herself. He wanted to help her, but he had to remain in disguise until he had proof of the smuggling. *Oh Lord, protect her*, he pleaded. A few others boarded.

*  *  *

Angelique saw an old man with a cane. She suspected that it was Buck but couldn't be sure. She knew he got the information and would be there somewhere. Her eyes watered from the tight grip Mr. Kennedy had on her. She kept quiet even though she wanted to scream from the pain. Screaming would only worsen her predicament.

"Where are we going?" Angelique asked to sound like she did not know.

"Shut up! You know too much already, Miss Nosy!" he bellowed.

"Can you let go, at least?"

"I said shut up!"

He slapped her face. She cried but quickly stopped herself. Buck grabbed the rail to keep from charging at Kennedy. The boat set sail. Mr. Kennedy held Angelique with one hand and the wheel with the other. He headed down river toward the Delaware Bay. Once in the bay, he turned off the lights and sat in the water. The rain tapped at the deck.

"We'll wait here for an hour or so and then turn back. We're going to the top deck," Kennedy announced. "You get moving up stairs!"

She stumbled up the steps. They were slippery from the rain. She tried everything to loosen his grip on her but had no luck. Occasionally, she kicked him, and he retaliated with a punch in her back. *He's going to kill me. If he finds Buck, he'll kill him too*, Angelique thought. On the top deck, Angelique swayed and got dizzy. She looked at the black river. She remembered the black flood that took her father and her fear of water came back. She felt sick. Mr. Kennedy threw her on the ground. She skidded across the deck and slammed into a door. He pointed the gun at her again.

"I am going to do what my helper wasn't able to do. Kill you right here but before I do, I have to wait on some folks," Kennedy said.

Angelique said nothing. Her mouth was dry. Her palms sweated. Her head pounded from slamming into the door. Her arms were filled with goose bumps. She took short, staccato breaths. *I hope Buck finds me in time.*

* * *

Buck crept up the stairs. He was careful not to let his cane or his steps give away his position. He needed Mr. Kennedy not to know he was there. Buck stayed in the shadows. He could see Mr. Kennedy with his gun pointed at her chest. Buck held his gun in his hand that did not hold the cane. Buck shed a small tear when he saw Mr. Kennedy slam her against a door and said a silent prayer. *If we get out of this alive, I'll give a sizable donation to the Church*, he thought. Buck was unaware that the door of the closet on the top deck opened a crack. He heard a churning noise on the water. The blackness of the water prevented him from seeing what was there, but he knew it had to be a ship. A small boat with its lights off headed toward Kennedy's ship. The small boat stopped its engine when it bumped Kennedy's. Buck shifted slightly to see and get proof of the smuggling. Mr. Kennedy let down a rope ladder. Five people looking frightened climbed the ladder, followed by three men and several packages.

"Get them locked in the hull before anyone sees them. I will take them to Rosetta to process," Kennedy said.

"Where's the money?" one man yelled back.

Kennedy threw a briefcase at the man who had scars on his cheeks and a few teeth missing.

Bang!

The gunshot rang through the air startling Buck so much he dropped his cane and lost his wig. The cane dropped with a loud thud. Buck cocked his gun. Angelique gasped when she recognized him. Mr. Kennedy looked around at the noise and looked for the gun.

"I'll take that money," yelled Enrique Bañal. He had shot the man with the missing teeth. "And the drugs."

"You left on a plane," Kennedy said shaking.

"No. I sent my brother on that plane. My sister has put herself at risk without payment for too long, Kennedy. The money and drugs now!"

Kennedy picked up the briefcase and threw it over Enrique's head.

Bang!

Another gunshot, this one from Buck's gun hit the briefcase to open it. Money flew everywhere. Everyone jumped. Buck leaped back into the shadows. Angelique seized her chance to get away. With all her might, she knocked over Kennedy and ran for the stairs.

Bang!

Kennedy's gun shot at Angelique. She skidded just barely missing contact with the bullet. Buck grabbed her.

"Let me go," she screamed.

"Shhh," Buck said. "It's me."

"Oh," Angelique whispered.

However, her screams forced Enrique, Mr. Kennedy and the two men to look toward the shadows.

Buck sprang into the light and yelled, "Freeze."

Before he could say FBI, more gunshots echoed through the night. They ricocheted off the railings and sides of the boat from every direction. Buck's gun shooting bullets as much as the others.

Buck danced away from bullets. Enrique aimed at Kennedy and Buck in turn. Angelique found a fire extinguisher and grabbed it. She sprayed the deck where Kennedy and Enrique stood, making both lose their footing. Kennedy got up and lost his gun. He grabbed Buck. He and Buck stood locked arm in arm struggling to hurt the other. Buck desperately clung to his gun, but let go of his cane. They headed for the railing.

"You're not going to push me over the railing again, Buck screamed and tightened his grip on Kennedy.

Angelique suddenly realized how Buck got injured. She noticed his injured leg wobbling under Kennedy's weight. Enrique continued raining bullets at them, but his aim was poor because of the heavy rain. He missed their ears by inches.

"Oh yeah? We'll just see what happens to nosy managers."

"I have news for you. I may have an MBA, but I'm no manager."

"Yeah 'cause you're dead."

Kennedy began throwing him overboard. Thinking fast, Angelique threw the fire extinguisher at Kennedy. At the same time, two bangs rang through the air. One came from Buck's gun. The other came from another agent reaching the top deck. Angelique screamed. Kennedy fell overboard. Enrique fell to the deck. Buck collapsed. Two guns hit the floor. The rest of the crew held up their hands. Angelique ran to Buck.

"Are you all right?" she asked with panic. "Please God, let him be all right. Buck. Buck," she cried. "I love you."

Buck opened his eyes. He smiled at her. "I'm just in pain. I'll be OK. Get my cane, please."

She raced over to the cane and came back. Buck stood although wobbly.

# Chapter 34
## *The Double Cross*

"Angel, are you OK?"

"Yes. I'm fine. Just a little sore. I'm not afraid of the water any more. My true love did not die like my father. I don't mind you keeping this job."

"Angel, I don't need this job any more. I suspect the company will be sold. Roxy will have to find a new job."

"She can work for me. I need a cook. At least, until I go bankrupt. What do you mean, you don't need this any more?"

"I am Special Agent Buck Robertson. I work for the FBI. I was undercover here. We thought Kennedy was doing illegal activity."

"You are?"

"Yes. The day I was hurt in the water and a police officer risked his life to save mine, I knew I wanted to be one too. My business degree gave me an advantage at the FBI Academy so I went there instead of NYPD. I'm in the embezzlement and credit card division. We thought Kennedy was embezzling to fund illegal activity. But, until we had evidence, I couldn't tell you the truth."

"But Enrique…"

"Apparently, Kennedy was double-crossed. The way I see it, Kennedy used Enrique's sister as a place to put the illegal immigrants. She got them illegal work but did not get paid. That got Enrique mad. He kept a record of all the illegals in what I thought was a writer's manuscript. He threatened Kennedy with exposure. Kennedy was one step ahead of him, though. He told Enrique to come after you, sabotage your plumbing and blame me or he would tell the authorities he set the fire on the retirement community."

"How do you know all this?"

"Some of it, I deduced on my own. Some of it, I learned from Trixie, Kennedy's girlfriend. After I got your letter, I visited her. She gladly told me what she knew when I reminded her she could go to jail for conspiracy to commit murder. But, I also found out she protected herself too."

"And the ones who caused the car accident?"

"They're gone. They took Kennedy's advice and disappeared shortly after the night you and I were hurt. I figured out that Kennedy was the man who attacked me that night."

Buck changed the subject. "Why did you say you're going bankrupt?"

Angelique released the tears she held back all night.

"I can't make ends meet. The sabotage, the putting up the fire refugees and the free stays of your relatives have killed me financially. Not to mention the hospital bills I had to pay for out of my pocket. I'll have to close the inn, the dream of my parents."

The tears poured down her face. Buck felt sorry for her, but he remembered the agents, criminals and illegal immigrants.

"We have to get this ship back to the pier."

Coming to her senses, Angelique agreed and headed toward the helm. She and Buck held hands and steered the ship toward Penn's Landing. Buck phoned his office and Coast Guard informing them of what happened.

"Buck when we get to the dock, a reporter will be there. I tipped her to a story of smuggling in exchange for a prominent story about my inn. Is it Ok to answer her questions?"

"It should be. The case is now closed. The Coast Guard will find Kennedy's body."

They were silent heading toward shore, but Angelique still shed tears. The rain slowed to a drizzle.

# Chapter 35
*Back in Business*

The paramedics tended to Buck's leg. His ligament split again because of the weight he put on it. The flying bullets grazed his skin. He was fine. He told the reporter all he could remember. Angelique had bruises on her arm and face. The swelling in her cheeks reminded her of getting numb for filling cavities. Her fingers had scratches and scrapes. Her heart pounded but slowly returned to normal.

"You'll be OK," the paramedic said, "But to be safe, we're having your head checked at the hospital."

Angelique sobbed. She thought about more hospital bills she could not pay. Buck put his arm around her and kissed her.

"Sir," someone called.

"Yes," Buck answered.

"We found money. We searched every ship and your office," the short colleague said.

"Great. It's evidence. Send it to the lab."

"Not sure, it's evidence. This money was stolen from Miss Chalfonte."

"Stolen from me?" Angelique asked looking puzzled. "The money I lost wasn't stolen and that was before all this happened."

"We arrested Trixie for extortion. She had blackmailed some clients. She admitted to taking money from Miss Chalfonte. She had pretended to be a guest and found the safe. She emptied it. So we're giving it back to you, Miss Chalfonte."

"Maggie told me she deposited that money. I guess she forgot. Why was it at the touring company?"

"Trixie worked with Kennedy setting up his alibi and trying to get her to seduce me to frame me for your murder," said Buck.

"He probably needed cash for one of his plans and told her to get it any way she could."

"That makes sense. How much is there?"

"50,000 dollars," the young agent said.

"That's enough to pay a couple of months' bills. After that, I should be able to sustain my business," Angelique said.

She wiped her eyes, dried her face and smiled.

"Angel, my relatives sent a thank-you note to me when I was on crutches. They said they appreciated your kindness in times of grief. All of them plan to visit your inn for Freedom Week, pay full price and bring many friends. Also, my Uncle Joe is a columnist for the *New York Post* and will do a feature on the 1776 Inn and recommend it for tourists to Philadelphia," Buck explained.

Tears of joy filled her eyes.

"God always repays kindness tenfold," the young agent said.

"One more thing. I promised God if you were safe, I would donate money to the Church. Do you know where I can put my inheritance from Mom's death?"

"Give it to Sister Maryanne at the St. Vincent de Paul Society shelter. She was going to allow me to stay there that night. She stayed at my side many nights after that in the hospital."

"Will do. But, you will get some too. I love you so much. I will never leave you. I want to marry you."

"I thought you couldn't marry me."

"That was because I was undercover and I couldn't tell you the truth. I also didn't want you in danger, but you ended up in danger anyway."

"Oh Buck. I love you too. I want to marry you too."

After being checked by the hospital, Angelique went home to more good news.

"Miss Angelique. Ah so glad you're safe. Ah so glad you're home. The phone's been ringing off the hook since ya left last night. People got ya mailing. They want ta come here," Maggie shouted.

She jumped up and down. Angelique beamed with happiness.

## *Epilogue*

In the months that followed, Angelique's inn flourished thanks to the mailing, the column, the article in the magazine, Buck's family recommendations and word-of-mouth. Buck and his father moved into the inn. He remained at the FBI. They were happy beyond their wildest dreams. Maggie stayed with the inn and was happy to be a housekeeper and friend to Angelique who had hired Roxy to cook. She had gone to culinary school at night while working for the Delaware River Touring Co. The breakfasts she cooked for Angelique won her awards and brought people to the inn regularly.

Buck and Angelique got married at a ceremony at the inn on July 4. It was partly a publicity stunt but Buck's family was already there. Buck took his bride to Angelique's suite.

"Now, Angel, I can do what I wanted to do long ago."

"Yeah? What's that?" she teased.

"Just this."

He scooped her into his arms, laid her on the bed and kissed her passionately. She was not afraid and kissed him back. Buck slowly removed her clothes and explored her legs until he came to her vagina and silky hair. She was ecstatic. She could not feel the bed beneath her. She danced on the clouds. Buck raised her shirt over her head and kissed her abdomen and her beautiful breasts. He grabbed one breast, gently rubbing it.

"Oh Buck!" Angelique screamed.

"Angel, I can't stop now if I wanted to."

"I need more."

Buck continued. One hand inside her and one hand cupped to her breast. With his tongue he circled the nipple on the other. Angelique's hands moved. They inched their way up Buck's shirt. She felt the hot chest underneath. She played with his chest hair. He moaned and tightened his grasp on her nipple. Her fingers traveled to his groin. She carefully slipped off his underwear. Her delicate fingers rubbed his private area. Buck moaned again. She felt the hardness and then gazed into his eyes. They were glazed as if in a dream. She lifted his head from her breast. She pushed him on his side. It was her turn to taste sweet nectar. She licked his nipple, teasing with her tongue. Buck couldn't breathe. Her tongue slid down to his groin. She tasted it, which sent shivers down Buck's spine not to mention hers. Angelique stayed there, licking and tasting until she knew he was ready. Buck rolled over. His body covered Angelique's.

"This will hurt a little, Sweetheart."

She nodded.

Buck pushed inside her. A wave swept over both of them. Neither could think. They had reached eternity together.

"What a way to start our honeymoon!" he exclaimed.

"Mmmm," was all she could say.

They left the next morning for a cruise in the Caribbean. Angelique decided that would be the perfect honeymoon. She no longer saw the danger of the Delaware River or any water. All she saw was calm waters for sailing.